Murder at Woodley Grange

John Tallon Jones

Penny Detective 13

D1446935

Published by G-L-R (Great Little Reads)

Copyright G-L-R

All rights are reserved, and no part of this publication can be reproduced in any format without the written consent of the copyright owner. This includes but does not limit mechanical and digital devices, photocopies, or audio recordings.

All characters described in this book are fictitious, and any resemblance to actual persons either living or dead is coincidental.

TABLE OF CONTENTS

Winter 1988

CHAPTER ONE

"I knew that there was going to be a catch."

Cynthia repositioned her head on the pillow so that she was facing me. "Go on," she said.

"Well, it was just that I thought we had something special between us."

She sat up, and her long black hair fell seductively over her naked shoulders. "Something special?"

"Well, yeah. That's what I thought."

"So tell me, Morris; when do you ever phone me up unless you want to get me into bed?"

"Er... I do take you out sometimes."

"You have never taken me out, Morris."

"What about that Italian restaurant in Bootle last Easter?"

"Being asked to leave an establishment because the person you are with is banned hardly constitutes being taken out."

"Oh yeah, I forgot about that." I laughed feebly and felt my face reddening.

"Just like you seem to forget my telephone number unless it suits you."

"This time, I feel like it's you that is using me, Cynthia."

"So you admit that you take advantage of me?"

I wasn't going to admit to anything, so I kept my mouth shut.

"I have never used you, Morris. I use things like my credit card to buy a hamper from Fortnum and Mason for instance or to book a holiday in the Caribbean. I hardly think that asking you to perform a small favour amounts to me using you. I want to hire you in a professional capacity, which is a little bit different in my eyes."

"So are you going to pay me?"

"In money or in kind, Morris?"

She was trying to make a joke, which considering she had no sense of humour was a joke in itself. I sighed internally. "Which is better for you?"

She sat up in bed and turned her violet eyes on me. She knew I could never resist those.

"In kind will do, I suppose."

She leaned over and kissed me. "Do you want a down payment?"

"Go on then; we can work out the instalments after."

Later, when we were having one of those cigarette moments, without the cigarettes, I realised what I had done. I had reached a new low in my career. Now, I was working for sex. It dawned on me that I was going to have a problem with my partner Shoddy. How was he going to get his cut? I looked at Cynthia, lying in my arms like a contented feline, and shook my head at the thought that had just passed through it. No, she would never consider that, and to be honest, it would be a little perverse. The only solution was not to tell him. That would be another new low in my career as well. Lying to my partner.

Cynthia sat up, put her arms around my neck and kissed me passionately on the lips, then started nibbling my ear. From experience, I knew that she was probably ready to carry on but twice was as much as I could manage, even though she was possibly the most beautiful and sexiest woman I had ever met. Even I had my limits.

She had the thinnest and most desirable body and knew how to use it to its full effect. I'm six feet four inches, but she was almost as tall, with legs that seemed to carry on forever, long black hair that reached her waist and skin so white that it was almost translucent. She had, however, a flaw that I found it hard to get over. She took everything so literally it was difficult to hold a conversation.

To take her mind off abusing me, I brought up the subject of the reason she had called me.

"So, show me that letter again."

That seemed to do the trick. She reached over to the bedside table and passed me a single sheet of expensive writing paper. It was so thick; it was almost like parchment. I wriggled out of her arms, sat up, and turned on the bedside lamp. She was tickling my stomach, now, and kissing my chest playfully. I tried to ignore her, but it was difficult. "When did you receive this?

"Yesterday."

At the top of the paper was a crest of arms. It had been typed, so it was easy for me to read.

Dear Cynthia,

I'm sorry that you were unable to come down to see us the other weekend as I could have explained in person. I did not mean to be rude about the money, but I have to draw the moral line in the sand somewhere, old fruit.

Things are going ghastly wrong, old girl, but you have already helped more than enough. I have made a grave miscalculation on the cash-flow side and to put it succinctly we have run out of money.

What can you do with a half-built roller coaster and a couple of children's rides? The answer is not a lot I'm afraid. There are those awful Americans coming over soon with the promise of investing dollars in the scheme, but I am not optimistic. Like I have said on numerous occasions before, though, I will not take any money off you, so don't even consider it. I am a gentleman, and like all good gentlemen, I am prepared to go down with my ship. Metaphorically speaking and all that.

I can honestly say that I have never been at a lower ebb. We need a miracle with the project, but please don't insult me again with any offer of funding because it makes me more depressed. Now, it is a case of physician heal thyself.

Tinkerty Tonk, old girl.

Binky.

Probably, the first problem I had with doing Cynthia this favour was dealing with somebody called Binky. "Doesn't he have a real name?" I asked.

"Really, Morris, you are an inverted snob you know. Everybody calls him Binky."

"Yes, but what is his real name?"

"It's Elliot Ponsonby Maximilian-Rothchester the third."

"Binky it is then."

She seemed to have lost interest in being playful. She lay back down on the pillow and pulled the covers up to her shoulders. "So, are you going to help, Morris?"

"Go through it again for me. It sounds easy."

"It is easy, Morris. I have known Binky since I was a little girl. The family never had that much money, but they have a bloodline that goes back to Charles the First."

"Wasn't he the one who had his head chopped off?"

"He was, Morris, but the Maximilian-Rothchester family managed to keep their land by changing sides just before."

I liked the sound of him already. The fact that Cynthia said that the family didn't have any money, meant nothing. She thought that people who only had ten bedrooms in their house were paupers. I guess that this attitude was one of the downsides of being a multi-millionaire if there were any. "So what do you want me to do?"

"Well, Binky and his family wanted to convert their estate into a fun park. Binky had this idea for it to become the English Disneyland. Unfortunately, he didn't realise how expensive it was going to be. He has used up all of the funding, and almost bankrupted the family. I have never seen him so low, but he is a dying breed of English gentlemen, I'm afraid. He will not borrow money off a woman. That's where you come in, Morris."

"So you want me to go there, pretend to be a prospective investor, and give him the funding he needs."

"That's it, Morris. Just go there. Have a meeting and give him the money. Even you can't get that wrong."

"So how am I supposed to explain myself? I was just passing his house and thought that he might need some cash?"

"I said that he wouldn't take money from me. If I tell him that I have a business associate that wants to get rid of some money to keep under his capital gains tax allowance, he will jump on you."

"But I don't understand all that rubbish about capital gains tax and all that."

"Neither does Binky, Morris. Why do you think that they are in such a mess? Binky is a lovely man, but couldn't even spell his name until he was fourteen. That's why we called him Binky?"

"So you are saying that he isn't clever?"

"I would go further than that, Morris. I would say that he is unbelievably brainless."

"But nice."

"Yes, yes, Morris. He is brainless but nice. I'm sure that you two will get along fine."

He sounded like my kind of business partner. "So how do I know how much to give him?"

"Just give him what he asks for. Let me know; I will have it ready within a week."

"This job sounded better and better. I lay down on the pillow. "So these instalment payments, will they be weekly or monthly?"

She dropped the covers and leaned over and kissed me. "I was thinking more in terms of nightly, Morris. Is that OK?"

"You drive a hard bargain, Cynthia, but I guess it will have to be." I reached over and turned off the bedside lamp.

CHAPTER TWO

As with most things that Lady Cynthia Laval put her hands to, events moved pretty quickly after that. Before we had a chance to get out of bed, she had phoned up Binky to tell him the news. Apparently, he was hunting deer in the Cumbrian countryside and wouldn't be back for a couple of days. After a long conversation with his wife, Roxy, it was arranged that I set off by train for Cumbria the next day and that a message would be sent telling him to return home.

"Roxy said that they would send a car to pick you up at the station," said Cynthia, climbing out of bed and starting to get dressed.

"Don't any of your friends have proper names? What sort of a handle is Roxy?"

"It's short for Roxanne, silly. Besides, I think Roxy is a rather cute name. A lot better than Cynthia."

"I thought hunting deer was banned in England."

Cynthia raised her eyes to the ceiling. "These animals need to be culled for their own good. People like Binky are doing them a favour."

"Yeah, I'm sure the poor animals are very grateful. Just like foxes enjoy having their throats torn apart by a group of bloodthirsty dogs."

"If you have never been fox hunting, Morris, you shouldn't pass judgement. It's part of our heritage and should be preserved."

"Just like slavery."

"What?"

"Slavery was part of our heritage until somebody banned it." I could see from the far away expression on her face, that I wasn't getting through and I was right.

She changed the subject. "I told Roxy that you were a business man that I knew, who had money to invest. She was so excited, Morris."

"Yes, but why do I have to go tomorrow?"

"Tomorrow is Friday, and Roxy is throwing a weekend house party for a few friends. She said that when he gets back, she will surprise Binky by telling him that you wish to invest. According to Roxy, it is not a moment too soon, as there are creditors sniffing around already. The hunting trip was his way of relaxing"

"So where is the house?"

"I would hardly call it a house, Morris. Woodley Grange is just outside the village of Woodley, in Cumbria. Binky is the Third Earl of Woodley."

"Naturally."

Cynthia glared at me. "Binky is the Earl of Woodley, but never uses the title as he thinks it's a bit tiresome and ostentatious."

"And how many rich snobby types will be there?"

"Apart from the family I don't have a clue who will be there, but don't worry; I told Roxy you were rather uncouth and didn't have any breeding."

"Thank you, Cynthia; that was very kind of you."

"Don't mention it. Now you don't have to try to fit in. You can just be yourself. They will love you because you are rich. The family has aristocratic blood in their veins but no money in their pockets. Your presence will be like a breath of fresh air.

Great! I was looking forward to it already.

Twenty-four hours later, I was stepping down from the slow mail train onto the platform of the tiny station at Woodley. I had told my partner Shoddy that I was going away for the weekend with Cynthia and he didn't give it a second thought. The fact that I had lied weighed heavily on my brain, but not so heavy that I didn't take advantage of two instalments off Cynthia before I left. Sometimes I wondered who was taking advantage of who in our off-on relationship. I think she saw me as her bit-of-rough on the side, but it didn't bother me.

There should have been somebody waiting to pick me up, but I was alone on the platform. Outside the station, the road was deserted as well. I picked up my duffel bag and was just about to ask the porter for directions to the Grange when I saw an old-fashioned Rolls Royce approaching.

The car trundled gracefully to a halt alongside me, and a woman in horn-rimmed spectacles stuck her head out of the driver's window. "Are you, Morris Shannon?"

"I put on my most friendly face. " I am indeed. You must be my lift to Woodley Grange. Nice motor."

"I'm Vanessa Tate. I work for Lord Rothchester. Throw your bag in the back and climb aboard. I hope that you haven't been waiting long, only I couldn't get the car to start."

I did as she said and got in beside her. She was a plain looking girl with mousy brown hair and facial skin care problems. The thick Magoo glasses didn't do her any justice either, or the heavy tweeds she was wearing.

She just about managed to engage first gear, and we sort of hopped down the road for a few hundred feet, before she slammed the engine into second and we shot off at speed. Her driving was so erratic that I was thrown back in my seat. I searched for a seatbelt frantically.

"We don't have seatbelts, I'm afraid. This car was built in the days that you didn't legally require them."

I smiled nervously and settled down into the plush red leather seat. She clunked noisily into fourth and kept to a steady twenty-five miles an hour, which I suppose was just as well. At least if she crashed at this speed, I wouldn't be hurled through the windscreen.

"Are you a nervous passenger, Mr Shannon?"

"Why do you ask?"

"Oh, I don't know. It's just the way you are gripping the seat. Your knuckles are turning white."

I released my grip and folded my arms. "Is that better?"

She laughed. " I know that I don't drive this monster very well, but I'm OK in my vehicle."

"Oh really? What have you got?"

"Nothing special. Just a little red Mini."

"This is a fine looking car, though."

"But it was built for another age. I think, Roxy... Er, Lady Rothchester would like to change. She's always borrowing my car to get about, but Lord Rothchester won't hear of it. Have you ever been to Woodley Grange before, Mr Shannon?"

"No, never," I replied. "Is it big?"

"It is one of the largest country houses in the North East of England. It's also one of the most beautiful."

I noticed that since we had left the village, there had been nothing but fields and winding roads. I hadn't spotted a building for at least ten minutes, though plenty of cows. "How far is the house?"

"Not too far now. I expect that you are tired after your journey."

"There is a lot of countryside surrounding it," I said.

She smiled to herself. "Yes, it can get a bit isolated, especially when it snows in winter. Still, one can't have everything."

"No, one can't," I agreed, with sarcasm that was way over her head.

We eventually came to the overpoweringly tall gates of the Grange, and she eased the car between them, though it was touch and go. After another long drive down a badly maintained track, we eventually emerged through a small wood, and I got my first glimpse of the building. Even I couldn't fail to be impressed by the size. Woodley Grange was at the centre of a huge park with perfect views in all directions. The house itself looked as if it had been added on to over the years, though probably not in the last fifty.

"The original building goes back to the reign of the Tudors," said Vanessa. "Of course, there is very little left of that but it is still classed as one of the top country houses in England, and it does blend in perfectly with the countryside around it."

She was right. If I was impressed, then it must be something special.

We drew up outside the main entrance and Vanessa stalled the car. She slammed on the brakes, and we came to an abrupt halt that almost dislocated my neck. It felt like I was suffering from third-degree whiplash. I vowed never to set foot in a vehicle that she was driving again and collected my bag from the back seat.

We were met at the door by a tall blonde haired girl. "You must be Mr Shannon," she said, holding out her hand. She gave me a ghost of a handshake and moved to one side to let me enter. I'm Lia. My Mum is resting, and dad is on his way back from murdering deer, so it's been left to me to show you to your room.

I looked at her face to see if there was any attempt of humour in her greeting and the quip about her father, but couldn't find any. She was certainly a bundle of laughs. She told me to follow her and set off at a brisk pace. I assumed by her actions that when she said for me to follow her, this was, exactly what she meant. I walked behind, and she never attempted to slow down or engage me in trivial conversation.

She took me up an imposing staircase and down a galleried landing. She opened the door of a bedroom, scowled at me and walked away without another word. The room was spacious enough and had a log fire burning in the corner. I went over to the window and drew back the heavy velvet curtains. The sun had just disappeared behind the mountains and had left a crimson sky in its place. It was growing dark quickly as it always did in the countryside. This was one of the reasons that I preferred the city. As always, I marvelled at the way rich people lived. It wasn't so much the money; it was the space that they had. Unlike my one bedroom council flat in Croxley, this building offered tranquillity and peace, with no noisy neighbours playing their ghetto blasters. I still wouldn't have wanted to pay the quarterly heating bill, though.

CHAPTER THREE

While I was musing about how great it would be to live in a mansion like Woodley Grange, the lights went out. Luckily, within a couple of minutes, I was rescued by a knock on the door. I stumbled my way across the darkened room with great difficulty, and when I opened it, Vanessa Tate was standing in the hall holding a lighted candle on a saucer. "Power cuts are something you get used to in Woodley Grange. Enrico is trying to fix the house generator. It shouldn't be too long."

"Enrico?" I enquired

"Oh, he's the general dogsbody around here. He does all of the jobs that keep the place ticking over. Rather like an old, loyal, family retainer, only he is not that old and not very loyal."

She told me that His Lordship would see me now in his private rooms and that she had been sent to show me where they were. I hadn't realised how thin she was until I saw her without a coat. I followed her back down to the first floor and then through a labyrinth of corridors that gradually got shabbier even in candlelight. The journey through the semi-darkness was surreal. It was like something out of a horror movie or a book by Charles Dickens. Bleak House sprang to mind.

She eventually stopped outside a door and knocked. A voice shouted, "Come in," and she opened it. "Here is Mr Shannon to see you, Lord Rothchester."

"Thank you, Vanessa."

The cold and damp hit me as I entered. The room was very dark and lit by a single candle and was like an icebox. From what I could see of Binky, he was an extravagant looking man in his mid-forties or maybe mid-sixties or early twenties. It was difficult to say in that light. He was wearing a black woollen hat that covered most of his head, and had a distinctive bushy black beard, and darting brown eyes. He was dressed in a Victorian smoking jacket, which was all I could see of him. He reached over his desk, avoided direct eye contact and pumped my hand enthusiastically. I assumed that somebody must have told him the news about the investment.

"Sorry about the temperature, old boy. We've got a spot of bother with the gas and electric tonight. Best wrap up warmly. Do you want to borrow a woollen hat? Thick hat and warm socks are the keys to staying warm."

I declined his offer, and he indicated for me to sit down.

Even in the semi-darkness, I noticed that like the corridor, the furniture in Binky's study had seen better days. There were double doors between two large bookcases. I assumed that this led to the rest of his little boy's play area. There were some odd-looking artefacts dotted around the room, but the focal point was a huge antelope's head on a wooden plaque nailed to the wall. It looked almost real in the mysterious light thrown out by the candle. Binky seemed to be oblivious to the ludicrous conditions.

"I see that you are admiring my head," he said. "I bagged that blighter in Senegal. I Got a couple of elephants and a lion as well that trip. Are you a hunting man, Shannon?"

"Er, no, not really. I'm more of a darts and pool player."

He let out a loud guffaw like a mule. "I'll see what I can do about organising a spot of deer hunting for us if you like. That's what I've been doing for the last few days. You are going to be eating one of the beasts over the weekend."

"Fantastic, Lord Rothchester."

He poured out two large glasses of whisky from a decanter and handed me one. "Please, call me Binky. Everybody else does."

I raised my glass. "Cheers, Binky. Did anybody tell you the reason why I'm here?"

"Yes, Roxy told me that you are a friend of Lady C. What line of business are you in, Shannon?"

I blurted out the first thing that came into my head. "Erotic ladies underwear."

He let out another guffaw and refilled my glass. "I wouldn't mind being in erotic ladies underwear myself. Especially Lady Cynthia's, but don't tell Roxy."

"Why? Is she jealous?"

"She would cut my balls off and feed them to the fox hounds if she caught me even looking at another woman. Roxy is a fiery girl. Have you met her yet?"

"No, not yet."

He drained his glass, refilled it and pushed the decanter over for me. "Help yourself, Shannon. I'm glad to see that you're a whisky man. I can't stand this new breed of young fellows that only drink cocktails. If a man drinks good whisky, then he is somebody you can trust."

I poured myself another generous portion. It was good stuff, and worth savouring. I took a generous sip, and let the flavour massage my taste buds before the liquid warmed my throat on the way down. I could grow to like Binky. Any man as generous with whisky as he was would make the perfect business partner. I began to wish that I really did have some money.

"So you are interested in investing in our new fun park."

"Yes, I have some money that I need to do something with. Cynthia spoke very highly of the project."

"I aim to be the number one theme park in England, then after that who knows?"

I decided to humour him. "Yes, Cynthia said you were very ambitious. How much do you need?"

"Don't you think that you should have a look at the construction work that we have done before deciding. I can take you around after breakfast tomorrow and then we can discuss a deal."

"That sounds good."

"In the meantime, Mr Shannon. Enjoy the evening. I have a few telephone calls to make, and then I will be out myself to join you."

He was indirectly telling me that the meeting was over. I got up, and he leaned forward, shook my hand, picked up a pen and started writing. I had been dismissed. I made my way to the door and walked back up the corridor, hoping I wasn't going to get lost.

Thankfully, Vanessa had lit a candle and left it on a table outside the door. I picked it up and stumbled around like a 19th-century tomb explorer. This house was a muddle of dark decaying splendour. It was chilly as well. I passed several old fashioned radiators that were not switched on and looked like they hadn't been used for years. About ten minutes into my adventure, the lights came back on, though in the corridor they were not that bright. I blew out the candle and stuffed the stub into my pocket just in case they went out again.

Eventually, after finding my way to the stairs, I made it back to my room. I lay down on the bed and thought about my encounter with Binky. For a man that was desperate for money to invest in his pet project, he seemed laid back. I would have thought that he would have bitten my hand off and made me sign a cheque there and then. Still, it takes all sorts, and his demeanour must have come from hundreds of years of interbreeding.

About twenty minutes later, after I had taken a lukewarm shower and changed my shirt, Vanessa arrived again to take me down for pre-dinner drinks. She opened the door of a room on the ground floor, told me to go in and mingle, and that she would see me later after she had changed. I entered the room self-consciously, as I had never been very good at making polite conversation.

"Who the hell are you?" Demanded an old man with a semi-balding head and an old weather-beaten face. He obviously had the same problem as me, when it came to being polite.

I simpered subserviently. "Morris Shannon. I've just arrived." I added, "I've been talking to Binky by candlelight."

"Have you indeed." He held out his hand. "I'm Sheldon Poole, Roxy's Father. The electricity is bloody awful in this house. We are not on the main grid system. Big mistake if you ask me, but then again, nobody asks me anything around here. Can I offer you a drink, Mr Shannon?" He didn't wait for a reply but handed me a glass of what looked like cooking sherry and walked off.

"Don't mind dad; I think he's going senile, though he always has been rude."

I turned around in the direction of where the voice came from. There was a small, slim woman dressed in a kaftan holding out her hand for me to shake. "You must be, Mr Shannon."

She was a cross between a punk and a catwalk model with exaggerated facial features and attention seeking bright red hair done up in a bob. If this was Binky's wife, then she was probably too much for the poor bastard to handle. She had what my mum called come-to-bed-eyes, and she was using them effectively on me. "Are you..."

"Roxy, Mr Shannon. Can I call you Max?"

"You can, Roxy, but my name is Morris."

She laughed politely at this, even though we both knew it wasn't very funny. "Well, Morris. Have you spoken to Binky about your investment offer? He was very excited when I mentioned it." She examined me intensely as if my answer meant the difference between life and sudden death.

I didn't want to let her down. "We spoke briefly, but he wanted me to go and look at the roller coaster tomorrow morning before we got down to any details."

She thought about what I said for a moment and nodded sagely. "Well, have another sherry. You can talk dreary business tomorrow. She turned to a sullen-faced man dressed in a crumpled seersucker suit who was standing behind her. There was an ominous space between him and the other guests and an air of depression that hung over his shoulders like a shroud. "Charles, this is Morris Shannon, he is here for the weekend to discuss business with Binky. Morris, this is Dr Charles Wellman."

The man stepped forward and thrust out a dry, bony hand. "Delighted to meet you, Shannon. He drained his glass and took another drink off a tray on the sideboard. "I hear that you are thinking of investing in Binky's little operation."

Roxy smiled at me and walked off, muttering something about getting Binky out of his study. I got the distinct impression that she was just using this as an excuse to get away from the doctor, and after five minutes conversation, I was desperately looking for a way out myself.

We had an embarrassing couple of minutes of protracted silence as if he was searching through his internal vocabulary of dinner party conversational gems. The best that he eventually came up with was, "So what sort of business are you in, Shannon?"

I was ready with the answer this time, though. "Buying and selling. Nothing very spectacular. My job is very boring really." I was going to add, a bit like you, but didn't want to sound rude.

"Have you any experience in pleasure parks?"

"No, but I'm willing to put money into any venture that is going to make a profit. Do you think that it would be a good investment, Dr Wellman?"

"Oh, I don't know anything about that. I'm just a village doctor. Entering into the world of business was never something I wanted to do. I'm sure that Binky knows what he's doing, though."

He lapsed into silence again and played with his ginger moustache in between studying his dirty fingernails, I saw Vanessa Tate talking to a couple of people in the distance, and I made a break for it. I didn't bother saying anything to the doctor, as I was pretty sure he was used to people just walking off.

"Hello again, Mr Shannon," said Vanessa. She had got rid of the glasses and changed into a low cut electric blue evening dress that emphasised her curves and stunningly thin waistline. It seemed that every time I saw her, she looked better and better. She had let her hair down, and her face had come alive. Either that or she had applied her makeup expertly. She saw the look on my face and smiled sexily. "I don't always wear tweeds you know. I was working when I picked you up; now I am relaxing. Have you met Alfred and Sky?"

"No."

"Alfred is Binky's son and heir, and Sky is his wife."

I could see the resemblance between Binky and Alfred. He had the same darting brown eyes, though without the bushy beard. Alfred had short greased back, long grey hair and thick black-rimmed glasses. I wondered what Sky could be short for, but thought it would be too rude to ask. Instead, I complimented him on the manor house, which seemed to cause the three of them some amusement.

Alfred lit up a Black Sobranie cigarette and blew several perfectly formed smoke rings into the air. "Woodley is such a big house to run. When I was a lad, we used to have servants, but now." He let his words hang in the air, and his eyes wander around the room. I could see what he meant. If you examined anything in this house with more than just a glance, you could see the decay and lack of upkeep. While it wasn't falling apart, just about everywhere could have done with a lick of paint and the furniture needed throwing out or burning.

I shrugged. "Maybe the new pleasure park will bring the money in to sort the place out."

He raised his glass. "I'll certainly drink to that, but every year that goes by it gets worse. Do you know that the radiators haven't worked for five years now?

"Yeah, I did notice that the place was a bit cold."

"A bit," laughed Sky. "You should be here when it snows. It's like living in a cave. We have icicles hanging from the ceilings."

My heart was bleeding for them. They should try and survive in my matchbox flat in Croxley. It was just as run down plus you had to deal with lowlife villains and drug addicts if you ever stepped out the door "So do you both live here?"

"We used to," said Alfred. "I bought a little place on the other side of the village, and we live there now. I can't say that I was too upset to leave the Grange. If I had my way, I would have sold the place off to one of those developer Johnnies and let them sort it out."

Sky was nodding her head like a donkey. She had the teeth and protruded chin that gave her an intense equestrian vibe. "Alfred and I have been trying to persuade Binky for years to sell. This place would make a divine hotel. All we get out of him is that the family has lived in the house for hundreds of years and he wasn't going to be the one to break with tradition."

Alfred interrupted. "And now the silly old sod has come up with the fun park idea."

"So you think that it won't be successful?" I asked.

"It's not that, old boy," said Alfred. "It's the thought of those awful people swarming all over the place with their unwashed children. I think I prefer to sell up than have the embarrassment of having to deal with them."

So, all had finally been revealed. Alfred was nothing but an upper-class snob with issues. I hated him already. He probably pigeonholed me as one of the great unwashed as well. "Yes, that does seem to be a problem for you, Alfred," I mused. "Still, at least if you do that, you might be able to afford to get your radiators fixed."

"Yes, old bean. I suppose you're right."

Just then the dinner gong rang, which was just as well the way the conversation was going.

CHAPTER FOUR

The sound of the gong booming around the house had given me the impression that dinner was going to be a fancy affair, but I couldn't have been further from the truth. The room where it was served was big but had a musty, damp smell and was unnaturally cold. The only heat was being thrown out by a very small electric fan heater, and the white tablecloth was stained and spotted with evidence of past meals. There were white saloon style doors at the far end of the room, and from the steam that was coming from behind them; I could only assume that this was the kitchen.

The place was set up like a fast food cafe. A young man dressed as a waiter emerged through the doors with a series of covered dishes, which he placed on warming hobs on the large dining table. He looked Italian or Spanish and had jet-black hair that was heavily greased combined with impenetrable black eyes and a pencil moustache.

"Have you prepared more food for the extra guest, Enrico?"

The man nodded, disappeared into the kitchen and came out with more dishes. "It's all out now, Mrs Rothchester. I'll just do the washing up before I go." He didn't sound foreign. I could have sworn that his accent was Newcastle.

"Yes, thank you, Enrico," said Roxy, who was sitting at the head of the table. As he disappeared back into the steamy kitchen, there was a general uncovering of the dishes.

"Not beefburgers again," said Alfred.

"I can't believe it, Roxy," whined old man Poole. Roxy's dad grudgingly forked three onto his plate, added potatoes, and vegetables, and poured himself a large glass of wine.

I reached over grabbed the bottle and poured myself one as well. I took a sip and almost spit it out in disgust. It tasted like lighter fuel. If this was how the aristocracy lived their lives, I was glad I was a commoner.

It was just as I noticed the empty seat, and realised that Binky was not with us that the incident happened. A loud bang like a car backfiring or a gunshot brought everyone in the room to a halt for a split second. They all stopped at different stages of eating or drinking something and then carried on as if nothing had happened.

It was Roxy that took control of the moment, and she shouted for Enrico. It took him ages to appear from the kitchen, but when he finally made it, she told him to go and get her husband and find out what he had been up to.

There was a smattering of laughter around the room. I seemed to be the only person in there that wasn't in on the joke.

"Are you not hungry, Mr Shannon?" Asked Sky, daintily putting a forkful of beefburger into her mouth. She had a face that looked as if a nosebag full of hay would have suited her better.

Alfred started laughing again. "I think we had better explain to Mr Shannon, Mother."

"Yes," said Roxy. "He has gone rather white. My husband's sitting room leads directly onto a walled garden where we grow our vegetables. There is also a chicken coop near the back door. We have a very large fox community around here, and Binky has a habit of lying in wait and blasting them through the window with his shotgun." She looked at her watch. "Usually around this time of night or sometimes even later."

"I do believe it's the only pleasure the old boy gets these days," added Dr Wellman.

This brought another smattering of laughter from around the table, just for the fact that the doctor had said something mildly interesting.

The smile was soon wiped off all of the faces, though, as we heard the sound of running feet. Enrico burst into the room breathing heavily, with a wild expression on his face.

"What's happened," said Roxy getting up from her chair.

"It's Mr Rothchester. He's been shot."

Lia screamed, Sky squirted ketchup over the tablecloth, and Alfred, Dr Wellman, and Roxy ran out of the room.

I followed at a more sedate pace but got lost on the way in the meandering corridors. I arrived at the door of his private rooms and walked in. There was no sign of a body, but one of the double doors was open, and Alfred and Roxy were coming out. They both looked in a state of disbelief.

Alfred blocked my way. "I don't think that you should go in there, Shannon. Dr Wellman is with him, so there is nothing much you can do."

"Nothing, any of us, can do, now," added Roxy, wiping her eyes with the back of her hand.

"It's all right; I've got experience of this type of thing," I blurted out.

"What? Do you see a lot of murders selling erotic ladies underwear, then?" said Alfred.

I saw what he meant. "What's happened?" I blurted out.

"The old man has been shot in his sitting room. We need to call the police," Said Alfred.

I followed them back into the main hall and listened as Roxy phoned the emergency services.

CHAPTER FIVE

By the time that I eventually got to bed, it was almost midnight, and I had a raging hunger. Looking back on the day, I realised that apart from a cup of tea and a bacon sandwich for breakfast, I had not eaten anything.

Binky getting shot like that had put an end to any opportunity of grabbing dinner and even I didn't have the nerve to approach Roxy and ask for a snack after what had happened to her husband. I sat in my bedroom, poked the amber embers of the fire and thought about the events of the day. I still didn't know much about what had happened to the poor sod. The police had arrived and cordoned off the area. It seemed that their medical examiner was our very own Doctor Wellman. He had been in the study with members of the crime team since they had arrived. Apparently, they were now waiting for a senior investigating officer to arrive from Newcastle, as the local police didn't deal with murders. Especially murder victims that were as high profile as Binky

That senior officer would not be arriving until the morning, but because everybody in the house had been in the dining room at the time of the shot, we all had alibis, so the police had left after sealing off the study.

Before I came to bed, I heard Alfred tell Vanessa Tate in a loud voice that the detectives suspected that the murderer had come in through the French windows of his private sitting room and had shot his father through the throat at close range. Sky had taken Roxy up to bed, and old man Poole had hit the whisky, after producing a bottle like a magician produces a rabbit from a top hat. The fact that he didn't offer me or anyone else a drink was typical of the man.

The shooting had put a whole new angle of my visit, and I wondered what I was going to tell the murder squad the next day. They were definitely going to interview me and check whatever story I told them. I put it out of my mind and turned my thoughts to eating. My watch said it was well after midnight. I wondered if there was any of the food left in the kitchen. With Binky lying dead in his study and the person who had fired the shot possibly still in the house, I didn't relish going outside my bedroom. I tried to go to sleep, but my stomach kept me awake with its constant rumblings. In the end, I got dressed, went out into the corridor and made my way downstairs. There was a dim light that had been left on, which gave the house a weird atmosphere. By the time I got downstairs, I was feeling more than a bit jumpy. The problem that I faced now was how to navigate back to the dining room and kitchen. One wrong turn in the semi-darkness and that would be it. I could be wandering around the corridors all night.

After a few false turnings, I eventually made it into the dining room, which as expected, had been cleared.

The kitchen was not much different. It was empty of anything edible. There was an alcove at the far end of the room behind a curtain with a large chest freezer. It contained nothing in particular, but I shuffled the contents around in the hope of finding something. Even a dish of ice cream would have been welcome. There was nothing in there that came close to resembling something I could eat. I would have to wait for breakfast. I grudgingly made my way back to bed. This was a very strange family with some bizarre habits.

On the way back to my room, I bumped into Doctor Wellman coming down the hall. He was carrying a tray with a decanter on it and blurted out as I went passed something about a nightcap after the awful tragedy. I nodded, smiled and said goodnight. I noticed that the tray had two glasses on it. I wondered who he was having his nightcap with. I went to sleep feeling sorry for myself and dreamt of fish and chips with sponge pudding for desert.

CHAPTER SIX

"So let's go through the main details of your story again, Mr Shannon."

I was sitting in a room that had been set aside for the police to talk to guests and family members. It made a pleasant change from the sterile police interview rooms in Croxley Police Station I was used to, and DCI Brian Foxley was trying his best to keep the atmosphere friendly. He was an unhealthy looking mouse of a man with unshaven, haggard features probably resulting from his early morning journey. His open-necked shirt and corduroy trousers looked in need of a good wash and ironing, and his manner was laid back and sarcastic. He gave the impression that there was a Detective Colombo type brain ticking away behind his half-moon spectacles.

I sighed internally and retold my tale for the second time. Even to me, it didn't sound convincing, and I could see by the look on his face when I had finished that the feeling was mutual.

"So this Lady Cynthia. Is she paying you money to be here? Is that what you are saying?"

Now that was a tricky question to answer truthfully. How could I explain to a man that looked like Foxley? He probably was still a virgin. "Yes, she hired my services to help out her friend."

"So how much did you charge?"

"We came to an agreement."

"What sort of an agreement."

"I'm sorry, Mr Foxley, but this is confidential client information that I can't divulge."

"So will this Lady Cynthia be able and willing to back up your story?"

"Yes, I'm sure that she will."

This seemed to satisfy him. He wrote something down in his notebook. "How well did you know Lord Rothchester?"

"I didn't know him at all. I only met him the once."

"And what were your impressions? Did he seem worried or anything?"

"I couldn't say. We talked a little bit, and he said that he was going to show me his rollercoaster the next day so we could discuss the investment."

"Ah, yes. The rollercoaster." Foxley flipped back some pages of his notebook. "The Rothchester family had been planning to turn part of the grounds into a pleasure park. Alfred Rothchester told me that they had recently got into difficulties with cash flow and that the firm that they had hired to build the rollercoaster had refused to carry on with the work. Is this correct?"

I shrugged. "I haven't got a clue. As I keep telling you, I only arrived yesterday. I met the family briefly and was sitting down to dinner when the murder took place."

He put his notebook into his pocket. "You say that you are a private detective, Mr Shannon. What is your impression of what happened last night?"

"I haven't got one. I was sitting down to eat, and everybody in the family except Lord Rothchester was in the room. We heard a shot, and the cook was sent to investigate. Could it have been suicide?"

"Hardly, unless he was able to kill himself, and then dispose of the gun. There were also muddy footprints entering from the French windows and going out again."

"I'm not sure what I have to do Mr Foxley. I am going to have to speak to Lady Cynthia, myself, to see if she wants me to give the money to the family now that Lord Rothchester is dead. Do you need to say anything about who I am?"

"I will need you to stick around for a while. I'm not going to say anything to anyone at this stage of the investigation, Mr Shannon." He stared at me hard and didn't return my rather nervous smile. "You're free to go."

I was free to go, but that freedom only extended to the house and grounds, if I was to believe what Foxley had said. I looked at my watch. It was almost two o'clock and no sign of anything to eat. I had got myself a cup of tea and found some biscuits for breakfast, but now my stomach was rumbling again. I strolled around the downstairs corridors of the house opening doors at random in the hope of finding family members sitting down to lunch. One of the rooms had a full-size snooker table, and another a makeshift gym with some lose weights and a rowing machine.

At the end of a particularly shabby hallway, I heard the sound of the radio coming from behind a door, and I pushed it open to investigate. The room was smaller than the other ones I had been in, but it was just as dilapidated and filled with old and ugly furniture. Sheldon Poole was cruising through stations on an old-fashioned valve radio. He glanced up and scowled.

"Oh, it's you. Don't they believe in knocking before entering a room where you come from?" He certainly was an unpleasant man.

"Sorry. Do you want me to go out and come back in?"

He reached into an antique cabinet and pulled out a decanter filled with what looked like whisky or brandy. He poured himself a generous portion. This room is probably the coldest in the house, Mr Shannon, but it has been designated as my parlour. I was thinking of getting a sign for the door to put off unwelcome guests."

"Good idea," I replied, turning around and heading back out.

"Just a minute. Did you want something?"

"I was just looking for where the food was being served. Has everybody eaten?"

The old man took a long drink. Reached out and refilled his glass. He held the decanter out. "Do you fancy a snifter?"

"I thought that you'd never ask."

I went over sat down and took the offered glass. I took a sip and winced. It was cheap whisky. Not even single malt but a blend. He saw the look on my face and laughed.

"I'm sorry. Unfortunately that was all I could afford. The family has fallen on hard times, and nobody listens to me anymore."

"How do you mean?"

"I mean Binky and his mad plans to turn us into Disneyland. I always said that Roxanne shouldn't have married him, but she went for the title. There is something rather grandiose about being called Lord and Lady Rothchester, don't you think?"

"I wouldn't know."

"Binky was never what you would call a great looker, and I could tell that he didn't have any money. Roxanne went for the breeding, but she was too proud to admit that she had made a mistake."

"So you think that the fun park was a mistake then?"

"All of that man's ideas to make money have been a mistake. He tried to organise show jumping; it fell flat on its face. Then there was the grouse shooting, which didn't have any grouse and the golf course with not enough land that was suitable. I could go on, but you see what I'm getting at, don't you?"

I nodded, and he refilled my glass.

"So what you are saying, Mr Poole is that Binky was not a very good businessman."

"I'm saying that Binky's biggest problem was that he was as thick as pig-shit. If the man had, two brain cells to rub together then I would have been very surprised. Roxanne, on the other hand, had a lot of good ideas that weren't so idiotic, but she just got shouted down."

"Oh yeah? Like what?"

"She wanted to sell the Grange to developers and let them turn it into a hotel, then share the profit. She even went as far as finding a company, but it was too much for Binky to get his head around. That stupid prick wanted to do everything himself and be the boss. I can't say that I am too disappointed that he is dead."

"So who do you think shot him?"

"How the hell should I know? All that I do know is that it wasn't me. It was probably somebody from the village with a grudge. Binky was always getting into arguments with the locals and owed money here and there. This is just my opinion, I might add, I never had a great deal to do with the fellow. Did Roxanne tell you that he wanted to kick me out?"

"No."

"He wanted to put me into one of these state-run old people's homes. Said that I would be better off. I ask you, what a moron." He drained his glass. "Anyway, let's go and find what's happened to lunch. I'm feeling a bit peckish myself.

He led the way out of the room and certainly could move fast when he wanted to. I followed him through corridors that had damp patches half way up the wall and bare wires where the electric plug sockets should have been. "Come on, Keep up!" shouted Poole. "These are the servant quarters. When I first arrived here, there were loads of the blighters; now we are down to just the one. He stopped abruptly at a door, and I almost clattered into his back. He knocked, and a man's voice answered from within.

"Who is it?"

"Sorry to disturb you, Enrico, but do you think that you could move your arse and prepare some lunch?"

After a short interval, the door was opened, and a bright-eyed and hot looking Enrico emerged in a green smoking jacket. "I was just having a nap. I didn't get to bed until late last night after what happened to Mr Rothchester, and all of the clearing up that I had to do."

His dark eyes flickered between Poole and me. I was right about his accent. He may have looked Spanish, but he sounded as if he was from the Northeast. He was also slightly out of breath, which didn't dovetail with the fact that he had been resting. I moved to the side of the door, and he altered his position to block me from looking into his room. He wasn't quick enough, though, because I caught a quick glance at what looked like a pair of red high heels

Enrico glared at me menacingly. He said, "I'll go and start to prepare lunch in a minute," and slammed the door in our faces.

As I made my way back up to my room, I couldn't help wondering who owned the shoes, and what she was doing in Enrico's room. This certainly was a very bizarre family.

CHAPTER SEVEN

It was a week after I arrived home and just around the time, I had put the whole incident of Woodley Grange out of my head that she turned up. I didn't recognise her at first because the punk look was gone, and I was knocked out by her clothes. She was wearing a tailored herringbone jacket with a black leather mini-skirt and fishnet stockings. She was taller than the last time we had met due to the shiny black stiletto heels. The bright red bob had been erased and replaced by a more effeminate blonde pageboy cut, which could have been a wig, but I wasn't about to ask.

Everything was different about Roxy as she stood waiting in the doorway like a high-class hooker on heat. Everything that is, except those come-to-bed eyes. The woman's sexual presence shone brightly from those two steely blue orbs that looked into you and beyond. They seemed to be daring you to make a pass, and her sensual mouth backed up the sentiment as she ran her tongue over her milk-white teeth. I felt like she was measuring me up and had already marked me down as inadequate.

I took in the new Roxy image as she stood there and let the silence stretch out between us like raw silk as I tried to figure out something smart to say. In the end, I just moved aside and let her squeeze herself suggestively past me and drop seductively into a chair. She still hadn't said anything, but the message she was sending out was very clear, she had come dressed to impress, and as I took my seat across the desk from her, I wondered what her game was.

"Mr Shannon," she said at last. "I'm sorry to have arrived unannounced, but it was a spur of the moment decision to come and see you."

"What can I do for you, Mrs...?" I couldn't remember her surname and felt my face growing hot with embarrassment.

"Please, Mr Shannon, call me Roxy. "

"OK, Roxy, what can I do for you. I assume that by now, you know that I am a private detective, and don't have any money to invest in the fun park."

"I spoke to Cynthia. Didn't she tell you?"

Now that was another long story. In my never-ending on-off relationship with Cynthia, we had recently been going through one of our off moments. I had only spoken to her briefly on the phone to describe what had happened. I think me mentioning the rest of the instalment package had something to do with her telling me she never wanted to speak to me again, and putting the phone down. Her last words had been to tell me that I was "A beast of a man with only one thing on my mind." I have to admit; I think that she probably was right.

"Mr Shannon?"

"Sorry, Roxy, I was miles away. No, Cynthia didn't tell me anything, but you are here now, so you can tell me yourself."

She answered after a pause. "I have recently had a shock."

"What sort of a shock?"

"It seems that somebody is trying to blackmail me."

"What? Like asking for money?"

"Not exactly."

Here we go again. Why couldn't I get a client who had a straight problem? I put on my most condescending voice, like a man who had nothing to lose. "If somebody is trying to blackmail you, by definition, they will always ask for money, or technically it is not blackmail."

"Well then, it's not blackmail it's more of a threat."

"What kind of a threat?"

She faltered and looked embarrassed. "It's a bit difficult for me to say. Can I trust you not to tell anybody?"

"I'm sorry Roxy, but if you need my help, then I can't do anything unless I know what exactly I can help you with."

"Cynthia did recommend you...but."

Looks or no looks, she was beginning to irritate me. "Maybe you think that you need a bigger detective agency. I can give you the address of a couple in Liverpool if you want."

"No, it's not that. It is just so hard for me."

I let the irritation show in my voice. "Maybe you can tell Cynthia what your problem is and she can pass the message on to me."

"Oh no, Mr Shannon, I couldn't do that. The fewer the people that know, the better. No, I think that I have come to the right person." She reached into her small black clasp bag and brought out an envelope. "This is what my problem is. I received this letter a couple of days ago. It is driving me crazy." She took a sheet of paper out of the envelope and handed it to me.

It was short and to the point:

Dear Mrs Poole,

I know what you have done, and you are going to pay for it, dearly.

The message was typed on a sheet of very cheap white writing paper.

"Poole?"

"My maiden name."

"Can I have a look at the envelope? " I asked.

She passed it over. It was addressed to Roxanne Poole, Woodley Grange, Woodley. It was postmarked, Woodley.

"Do you know many people in Woodley?"

She managed a sheepish grin. "Just about everybody, but I haven't got a clue about who could have sent it."

"What about why?"

She shrugged and examined my desktop. "I guess somebody in the village doesn't like me."

"Is there any reason that you can think of, why?"

She shrugged again. "I didn't think that I had any enemies in Woodley, but it seems that I must have."

"So have you done anything to cause someone to send you this letter?"

"No. Do you think it has something to do with the death of my husband?"

"Has it? You tell me, Roxy?"

"Look, Mr Shannon. I came to you this morning because I am worried. I haven't done anything wrong, but obviously, somebody thinks that I have, and I would like you to find out who. Is this the sort of work that private detectives do?"

"Have you tried the police?"

"No, I thought it wiser to come to you rather than involve them. Besides, I'm not convinced how good the police are at solving mysteries. I believe in going private when it comes to getting results."

I couldn't argue with that, though I had never heard anybody describe my services like that before. "So the police haven't found out who killed your husband."

"They haven't found out or likely to. The detective in charge of the investigation is nice enough, but doesn't have any answers."

"And you think that this note may be related to the shooting?"

"That's why I want to hire you, Mr Shannon. I still have a daughter living at home, and if there is a maniac out there trying to do us harm, then I want a name. Maybe then, I can go to the police. But first, I need evidence."

"My services aren't cheap, and there isn't that much to go on. It could take me a long time to come up with something."

"What you want to know is have I got the money to pay. Is that it?"

It was my turn to shrug. "I just don't want you to waste your money."

"How gentlemanly of you, Mr Shannon. If I have the money, do you have the time?"

She wasn't too much of a lady to arrange herself sexily on the chair to make her plea more appealing. I had a distinct impression that Roxy wasn't a lady at all. She crossed her legs, and I capitulated. I opened the drawer, pulled out a terms of service document and slid it across the desk to her.

"That is my daily fee, plus expenses."

She carefully examined it. "Your services don't come cheap; I hope that your results justify the money."

"Like I said before, you haven't given me a lot to go on, so I can't guarantee anything. If you want to think it over?"

"No, no, Mr Shannon. I did all of my thinking on the way down here." She went into her purse took out a fistful of banknotes and handed them to me. "When can you start?"

I looked at my watch. It was still early. "I can be in Woodley this afternoon. Is there any places to stay that you recommend?"

"You could probably get accommodation at the local pub. It's called the Rose and Crown. I believe that it's quite adequate."

She stood up, and I followed her to the door, opened it for her and watched as she walked up the hall and down the stairs.

When she was gone, I picked up the money and put it in my wallet. After talking to Roxy, I needed a drink.

In the street when I went down, the sky was overcast and the temperature was plummeting towards zero, as was my optimism about my chance of solving this new case. If it was cold here, then I

knew that Woodley was going to be even colder. I made a mental

note to pack my thermals and headed for the pub.

CHAPTER EIGHT

About an hour south of Kendal a sign informed me that I had to get off the M6 and head for Keswick on the A56. A drive, which would have normally taken just over two hours, had already taken me three because of slow-moving trucks, and my temperamental Riley Elf, which didn't like long distance travel. I had pushed the speed up to about 65 on the motorway but now was back down to an average of 40, due to slow moving tractors and the occasional shepherd with his flock of sheep blocking the road.

That's what it was like in this part of the world. My frustration gave me one more reason to add to the list of why I preferred cities to the countryside. After reaching the sleepy town of Keswick, I might just as well have tossed a coin to decide which route to take next. Town planners in this part of the world didn't believe in road signs, and the local inhabitants didn't look like reliable sources of information.

I arrived in Woodley more by pure luck than anything else, and the mood the journey had left me in had morphed into a little red devil on my shoulder. He was poking me with his pitchfork and whispering in my ear that I should return the money in my wallet to its rightful owner and go back home to Croxley.

The white cottages with their thatched roofs looked deserted, as did the time-warped main street that ran through the village. The voice in my ear was beginning to get angry that I wasn't following his advice, but salvation was at hand. I saw a sign that said the Rose and Crown.

I turned into the forecourt in front of an ancient-looking black and white structure, collected my overnight bag and got out.

Inside the lounge, a jovial-looking plump barmaid in white linen smock-top looked up from the very dark glass of beer she was drawing from an oak cask and gave me a dazzling smile. She glanced at my bag.

"Were you looking for a room for the night, sir?"

"I was, I still am, and I hope, to God, I've found one."

She laughed, touched her hair into place and flirted at me with baby blue eyes.

"Are you on your own?"

"Unless I get lucky."

She ignored this remark as an innuendo too far and went into her sales patter. "We have an enchanting single for ten pounds plus full English breakfast. How long are you planning on staying?"

"I'm not sure yet. Can I see the room?"

"Of course you can, Luv, and I'm sure that you will find it enchanting."

She took me up an old-fashioned wooden staircase and into a large room with a big double bed, a wardrobe, a table and three wooden chairs. Everything gleamed with cleanliness, and there was a pre-1940s retro vibe going on that couldn't be ignored. A heavy smell of furniture polish hung in the air, like an early morning lavender mist. On the wall behind the bed was a reproduction Monet, and in the corner was a washbasin and an old-fashioned iron radiator. Through the window, I could see the sun gently falling out of the sky, leaving in its place a miasma of fiery colours that tinted the mountainside burnt orange, behind a village that didn't have any right to have survived into the twentieth century.

She turned to me like a small child that was looking for approval from her father.

"I find it enchanting," I said and paid her there and then.

I followed her back into the bar, and she poured me a glass of excellent beer that she claimed had been brewed on the site for over five hundred years. I ordered a Glenfiddich single malt to accompany it, and relaxed. I could feel the trauma of the day drain out of my system, and I casually brushed the red devil off my shoulder and into my top pocket for another time and place. This would have been a perfect paradise location if it hadn't been for the inconvenience of having to work.

After resisting the temptation to make an evening of it and stagger to bed, I asked directions for Woodley Grange. When I mentioned the Grange, I felt her curiosity burn into me like the tingly sensation of static electricity. She tried to pluck up the courage to quench her inquisitiveness and I let her sweat. In the end, I put her out of her misery and told her loosely that I was giving an estimate for work and left it at that. Whether she believed me or not was of no concern, but in a small place like Woodley, the locals must listen to lots of gossip. If all else failed, I was determined to tap into the village tribal chitchat line, and the barmaid, whose name was Gwen, looked like a good place to start. She had already provided me with information on the best place to get dinner, and it was here that I was heading, to have a quick bite to eat, before continuing on to meet Roxy.

The establishment Gwen had recommended was an American Diner situated on the main road out of Woodley that headed towards Workington and Carlisle. As I pulled into the crowded car park, the glitzy silver fronted eatery, called the New Yorker, looked about as out of place in the Lake District as the Rose and Crown would have done in Time Square.

A poster on the door advertised Line Dancing every Tuesday and Friday, and inside, a woman in full cowgirl costume was singing about standing by her man. As I made my way to a podium with a sign that told me I had to wait there to be taken to my seat, I realised why the streets of Woodley were deserted. All the residents were in here. I was a bit dubious about what type of food was going to be served in a place that was authentically American. The closest that I had ever got to American culture was watching the Beverly Hillbillies, Kojak and I Love Lucy, on TV. I drummed my fingers on the plinth and waited for one of the waitresses to see me. In the end, a young girl dressed as a cheerleader came over and said "Howdy partner," in a heavy Scottish accent, gave me a menu and asked me to follow her.

I spotted them immediately as I made my way across the room. Roxy's daughter, Lia, was deep in conversation with the man who had done the cooking on the night of the murder. I remembered that his name was Enrico, and he had been the one who had discovered the body. I was about to say hello but realised that both of them had glanced up as I came towards them, and looked right through me. They didn't recognise who I was, but why should they have done? I was wearing my trilby over my bald head, and we had only met for the briefest of moments.

The waitress directed me to the table in a wooden booth behind them, and I sat down without butting into their conversation. I ordered a bacon and egg burger with fries and tap water, as the diner didn't have a liquor licence. I tuned the rest of the room out and listened to what they were saying. Enrico didn't sound very happy.

"Maybe you think I'm not good enough for you," he hissed. "What's going on Lia? Why so cold over the last week? If I didn't know better, I would say that you've got yourself another man."

"Is that all you think about, Rico? I've got a lot on my mind at the moment, and unlike you, I don't flirt with everyone I meet."

"What do you mean by that remark?"

"You know exactly what I mean. I'm not blind, and also, I'm not jealous, so you can flirt with who you want. Don't you have any emotions that don't come from inside your trousers?"

"You're a bitch. Do you know that?

"You're not clever enough to throw rhetorical questions around without thinking them through. A bitch is a female dog, and the only one around here that has the habits of a dog is you."

I could hear from the tone of his voice that the guy was beginning to lose his temper. I heard the sound of a cup slamming down on the table and Enrico's voice trembling with rage. He was trying to whisper but not succeeding. "You and your family think that they are so fucking superior; just because you've got a big house and speak with posh accents. You're in for a shock, Lia. I've got eyes and ears, and I know what's been going on." I heard the sound of a chair being pushed away and saw Enrico's head above the dividing wall of the booth. People in the restaurant were beginning to take notice.

"That's enough from you, Enrico."

In all of the commotion I hadn't noticed Lia's grandfather, Sheldon Poole, come into the restaurant. He was standing at the side of their booth, and his presence seemed to calm the situation down.

"I'm just on my way out," said Enrico.

"Not before I get an explanation as to why you were speaking to Lia in that way."

"Like I said, I'm on my way out. If you want an explanation, then ask her. I'm just the odd job man with no brain."

"You're not even the odd job man anymore, Enrico." Sheldon Poole spoke with calm and deliberately controlled speech as if he was used to being in command.

"So you're firing me?"

"Absolutely. I expect you to collect your things in the morning; tonight you can find yourself somewhere else to sleep."

The two men were now facing each other, so close that they were almost touching. Most of the people in the diner were as fixed on the scene as I was; wondering what was going to happen next. For the sake of the captivated audience, Enrico attempted to laugh, but it sounded hollow. The tension leaked out of the situation as quickly as it began. Enrico knew that he was beaten. He pushed passed the old man and exited through the door.

Lia got up herself, gave Poole a withering stare and whispered with controlled anger. "I could have sorted that out for myself. I'm not a child." With that, she exited as well. Sheldon Poole sat down, and the cheerleader waitress came over to serve him as if nothing had happened. He ordered T-bone with grits and mash potatoes, which made me wish I had too.

I ate my meal and made myself scarce. On the way out the waitress with the Scottish accent told me to "Have a nice day." I looked at my watch and told her that I would try my best. It was just after seven o'clock as I walked out into the car park, and felt the chill of a strong wind blowing off the mountains.

Poole hadn't recognised me either, for which I was glad. I laughed to myself as I started up my Riley Elf and headed for Woodley Grange. Enrico and Lia had left in such a hurry that they had forgotten to pay the bill. I would have liked to have seen the old man's face when he was presented with it.

CHAPTER NINE

As a drove along the B436 towards the Grange, it started to rain. It was light drizzle at first, but as I climbed higher into the more desolate part of the Cumbrian countryside, it got heavier. I missed the turning for the house and was halfway to Workington before I realised my mistake. I turned the Elf around and headed back for Woodley.

In the space of five minutes, the rain stopped, a three-quarter moon peeped out from behind the grey clouds, and I found the single track that would spill me out in front of Woodley Grange. I passed through the impressive gates and pulled up in front of the house. Even in darkness, it was just as imposing. There were a couple of cars parked in the circular drive. One was a flash looking BMW, and the other one was the old Rolls Royce that had picked me up from the station.

I climbed the marble steps and made my way to the front door. Something caught my attention in the corner of my eye, and I stopped myself ringing the bell. It was Lia. She was sitting on a bench outside some French windows, smoking a cigarette. Her head was bent back and resting on the wall, and her eyes were closed in quiet contemplation. I walked over. She gave no outward sign of seeing or hearing me until I spoke.

"Hello again, I'm looking for your mother."

"Sorry?" She opened her eyes and looked at me in complete surprise as if she had been asleep.

"My name is Morris Shannon; I was here a while ago; do you remember me?"

She gave me the sort of look that didn't need words to explain. "Do you have an appointment? Are you from the police?"

"No, I'm not from the police, but I do have an appointment. Is she in?"

"She's around somewhere, but I wouldn't know where. I've been out."

I resisted the temptation to tell her that I knew and waited to see if she was going to get up out of her seat and let me in. She seemed to be enjoying my annoyance like a spoilt little child. The lights of a car picked us both out for the briefest of moments before they were extinguished. I turned around and saw that a little red Mini had pulled up beside my Riley Elf. They made a fine looking couple. Lia's grandfather, Sheldon, and Vanessa Tate got out and made their way towards us. I noted that Poole was carrying a plastic bag with 'AMERICAN DINER' plastered all over it. He had obviously opted for the takeaway service.

Lia stumped out the remains of her cigarette as they approached.

"Hello grandfather, have you met...? What was your name again?"

I turned around and held my hand out. "It's Morris Shannon, Mr Poole; I'm here to speak to your daughter. Do you remember me?"

He embarrassingly ignored my attempted handshake, and I dropped my arm. I felt like head butting him for his arrogance. He looked me over with his tiny weasel eyes and then turned them on Lia. "I think that we need to talk, young lady. "Vanessa," he said to the woman who was standing just behind him. "Take Shannon into the house and see if you can track down mother, will you."

"OK." Vanessa took me by the arm and led me in through the French windows. Lia watched us go. Poole stood over her with both hands on his hips in a very aggressive pose.

We entered a room that I had not been in before. It was large and dimly lit, with a dark oak wooden floor and expensive looking scatter rugs. The furniture was heavy turn of the century Victorian. A shiny black concert grand dominated one corner, and the walls were hung heavy with old portraits of the Maximilian-Rothchester family through the ages. Even in oils, they looked like a weird bunch of characters, yet I could spot a definite family resemblance in all of them. They could all have been Binky with a different hairstyle, even the women. The beams that held up the fire blackened old ceiling were dark oak and matched the floor. There was a huge chandelier that hung down in the centre and tucked into the corner a marble fireplace that crackled and spat. The logs glowed red and threw out a fierce heat.

"Can I get you a whisky, Mr Shannon, while I go and see where Mrs Rochester is?" She walked over to a silver tray and poured me a large one from a Chrystal decanter. I prayed that it would be single malt that was at least half-decent and was wrong on both counts. These people either had no taste or no money. Maybe they didn't have either. Vanessa disappeared, and I sauntered over to a chair near the door and eavesdropped. I had stopped feeling guilty about furtively listening in on the lives of other people, years ago. It came with the job. I was paid to snoop around and pry into other people's business, so it was a professional thing. In this case, however, I was genuinely curious.

The straight back chair I chose had certainly not been created for comfort, but it was well placed behind the ornate ceiling to floor curtains for me to hear the murmured conversation very clearly.

"Why did you let that man talk to you like that, Lia?"

"I don't see what business it is of yours, grandfather, how I speak to my friends."

"Friend? This man is one of our servants. Do you mean to tell me that you don't know the difference?"

"Well, he certainly isn't a servant anymore, is he? You got rid of him tonight, so as he is no longer in our employment, using your logic, I guess that you can't have any further objections to me seeing him socially."

"He is hardly the type of person that you should be socialising with, Lia. Haven't you met any eligible young men where you work?"

"You really are a snob, grandfather. The days of master and servants are well and truly over with. It's a free world now, or haven't you noticed."

"That young man is after something."

"Well, it can't be our money because we haven't got any."

"I didn't mean that."

"What did you mean?"

A full minute went by of complete silence. The pause in the conversation was so long that I thought that they had both gone. Eventually, Poole spoke in a voice that even to me sounded very intimidating. "I'm warning you, Lia. Stay away from Enrico Cicero. There are things that you don't know about him. Bad things and I don't want you to get hurt." With that, I heard the sound of footsteps walking away, and the front door opening and slamming.

There was something about Sheldon Poole that made the hair on the back of my neck stand on end. He had all of the qualities of somebody that it wasn't a good idea to get on the wrong side of.

CHAPTER TEN

It was a good ten minutes after the conversation outside had ended that Roxy made an appearance. She was dressed in a low cut cashmere sweater and mini skirt. She saw the way I was looking at her and made a play of adjusting her cleavage to make it less accessible. The effect was the exact opposite, and I wondered if she knew. I made a comment about how nice this part of the house was, which she ignored. She poured herself a whisky, sat down on one of the high-backed chairs and examined me like I was a specimen from another planet.

"So have you started your investigations yet?" It was obvious that she now considered me to be the hired help.

"Not yet, it's a bit difficult knowing where to start. It could be anyone."

She went into her clutch bag took out an envelope and handed it to me. "This arrived this afternoon in the post. It was waiting for me when I got back from your office."

I pulled out a single sheet of paper and read it. It had the same typeface as the other letter.

Dear Mrs Poole,

You are going to pay dearly for what you have done.

I looked at the envelope. It was postmarked 'Woodley.' "So you don't have any ideas who it could be?"

"Of course I don't. If I did, do you think I would have hired your services."

I was wondering about that. "So why did you hire me and not somebody local?"

"You came recommended by Cynthia, which is all that I needed to know."

She made me sound like I was a bottle of wine. "OK, I can understand that you want to be discrete, and hiring somebody trustworthy from outside the area is the best way. Is there anything that you can think of that you may have done, which might have caused anybody to want to harm you?"

"No, of course not."

"Could it have anything to do with the death of your husband?"

"It might have done if I had murdered him, but I didn't. I want to think that it is somebody playing some awful joke, by trying to scare me. Do you think that I could be in danger?"

"I think that maybe you should go to the police."

"And get laughed at. No, I am happy at this stage to let you do some investigation and see if you can get an idea about who may have a grudge against me."

"Have you told anybody else about this?"

"No, and I don't want you to either. Don't you type of people have ways of getting information out of people without them knowing?"

"I think you are mistaking my type of people with hypnotists. You are not giving me much to go on."

"Is it a question of more money?" She started to reach into her bag.

"It's not the money; it's more a question of having my hands tied."

"So you are saying that you don't want to carry on."

"I'm not saying that. I wouldn't have made the journey if I wasn't going to give it a go. I think that the best thing for me to do is to pretend that I'm investigating the death of your husband. If I get lucky, I may find out some information as to who sent you the letters. I will also do some sniffing around in Woodley. It's a small place, so maybe somebody has information that is relevant."

"So what do you want me to do?"

"I would like to speak to all of the members of your family if I may. How about I start with your dad and Lia, tomorrow morning. Would that be possible?"

"Lia goes out very early in the morning. She works in a solicitor's office in Carlisle. You could see her when she comes back in the afternoon. You could talk to my dad in the morning if you like. He very rarely goes out before lunch."

I arranged to call back the next day and made my way back to my car. Somebody had turned out the veranda lights, and the car park was in darkness. With the heavy curtains drawn in the big house, there was no light pollution whatsoever, and the sky was lit with a million stars, though there was no moon.

About a mile down the road, my headlights picked out the figure of a man standing at a bus stop. As I was passing him, I got a quick glimpse of his face. It was Enrico Cicero. He saw me looking and stuck his thumb out hopefully. I pulled up sharply, and he ran and opened the passenger door.

"Thanks a lot, mate." I could smell the beer on his breath as he got in and sat down beside me.

"Cold night," I said.

"Yes, and the bus service is shit."

"Have you been visiting the Grange?" I asked.

He glanced sideways and looked at me curiously. "What makes you think that?"

"It's just that this road runs right passed the house."

"I used to work for the family that lives there."

"Used to?"

"Yes, the bastards fired me."

"Really! Why was that?"

He gave me another hard stare. "I've got no idea, mate. You'd have to ask them."

"So what did you do?"

"What didn't I do? I was cooking, driving them around, doing a bit of gardening and odd-jobbing."

"So what will you do now?"

"I dunno. I might go back to what I did before."

"What was that?"

"I was in the army. SAS."

"That must have been fun."

He didn't seem to like my attempt at humour. "That was no joke, mate; I was in the Falklands when we took back Port Stanley."

It was my turn for hard looks. The guy didn't look like he was Commando material, but looks could be deceiving I guess. He was either extremely tough or a bull shitter. I think the wise money was on the latter.

We went over a dip, as we joined the main road, which was the way back to the village. The road was mainly dark and although we did pass a couple of islands of light in the shape of houses, there hardly any other traffic. We went by a pub, with a sign swinging above the car park that said, The Slaughtered Dog. "Drop me off here," he said. "I could murder a beer. It's been one of those nights."

"What about getting back into Woodley?"

"No worries, there is a bus stop just down the road."

I turned the car around, pulled into the car park and stopped. "It's been one of those days for me as well. Do you mind if I join you?"

We walked through the car park, which only had a couple of vehicles, and pushed our way through a door marked, bar and smoke room.

The pub had a low ceiling with beams and a smoky fireplace. At a table in the corner, a couple of locals were playing cards, and there was a man nursing his drink on a barstool. The floor was scattered with sawdust, and a sign behind the bar said no 'no spitting and no credit.'

"Interesting place," I said. "What do you want to drink?"

He looked grateful that I'd asked, said that he would have a pint of bitter, and smiled. It was the first time that I had got a clear look at him. He had perfect white teeth, dark eyes and a Latin complexion. The little pencil moustache made him look like a spiv. I guessed that there was Spanish or Italian somewhere back in his bloodline, but he still didn't look old enough to have fought in the Falklands conflict. He was still just a pup, though a big one.

The barman approached us with the stealth of a ninja. He was a middle-aged man with a bald head and unhealthy looking skin.

"I've not seen you for a while, Rico. Where have you been hiding?"

"You know what it's like, Steve. No rest for the wicked."

"What can I get for you, gentlemen?"

I ordered two pints of local bitter and whisky, and he nodded his approval at my selection and moved away.

I took my trilby off and put it on the bar, expecting Cicero to recognise me from the dinner that he had cooked at the Grange. He didn't bat an eyelid, which made me wonder if at the time he had been too preoccupied with something else. Could he have been involved in the murder? Fortunately, it wasn't up to me to find that one out, but he was in the running for sending the threatening messages to Roxy.

When our drinks arrived, Rico downed his whisky in one and drained half of his beer before I had time to swallow a couple of mouthfuls. The drink seemed to ignite some happy spark inside him, and he wiped the froth off his mouth and held his hand out. "I'm Enrico, by the way, but you can call me Rico."

I took his hand and gave it a squeeze. "Morris Shannon. You can call me Mr Shannon."

The smile left his face for the briefest of moments before he realised I was joking. He finished off his beer and put his arm around my shoulder like we were old pals. "What do you say that we go on from here and make a night of it, Mo?"

"In Woodley? It's hardly the West End, Rico. What shall we do, find an all night tea room?"

"I've got it sorted, don't worry. I've got this tart called Gilda. She's a real swinger. She lives in the caravan park behind the village. I could give her a call from here and ask if she could get one of her friends around for you. What do you say?"

"I say that I need to get up early tomorrow so maybe we can schedule it in for another day."

"What's the matter with you, man? Don't you like to party?"

"Not really, Rico, but I'll have another drink before I go." I indicated for the barman to bring us the same again and this seems to pacify him.

He dropped his arm from around my shoulders and said, "Suit yourself it's your loss."

He drained his whisky and headed for the toilet. The barman watched his back disappearing through the door. He picked up a pint glass and idly started polishing it with a towel.

"I hope you don't mind me asking, but are you a friend of that gentleman?"

"Nope, never seen him before. Why do you ask?"

"No reason. He is OK most of the time, but he has a habit of becoming very aggressive after he has had a couple of drinks. Just be careful what you say to him." He looked me up and down. "You look big enough to handle yourself, but that fella would put a glass in your face if you didn't say hello to him in the right tone of voice."

"Bit of a troublemaker is he?"

"You could say that. He has never caused any trouble here, but he does have a reputation for violent behaviour in the village."

"That must be his commando training," I said, looking for a reaction.

The barman laughed. "If he's been a commando, then I'm an eccentric millionaire. I forgot to tell you that he's a liar too. If you believe what he says, he took on Argentina single-handed and is now working for the British Secret Service."

As he was talking, Steve the barman was cleaning his glasses and stacking them on a shelf. Without me asking, he refilled my whisky glass and said: "On the house." As I took a sip, the door opened, and a man in a grey windcheater and matching baseball cap entered the room. He had the sort of face that looked like it had never seen better days and the kind of expression that meant he was either a career criminal or a bent cop.

"Morris Shannon?"

"Yeah?"

"I clocked your vehicle registration in the car park, so I figured you were in here. That saves me a trip into the village. I'm Detective –Sergeant Floyd."

"What's the trouble, Sergeant?"

His thin, bloodless lips drew back into a kind of sneer and revealed the fact that he hadn't been doing regular checks with his dentist. "That's detective-sergeant, and I'm afraid it's the worst kind of trouble."

I saw Enrico come through the door, eyeball Floyd and go back to where he came from in one seamless movement. I waited to hear the bad news.

"I'm afraid that there has been an incident up at Woodley Grange, sir."

I didn't like the way he had called me 'sir.' "What sort of an incident."

"Mr Poole is dead. I was told to come and collect you and take you back for questioning. Are you going to come quietly, sir, or do I need to caution you?"

"What? Are you saying that Mr Poole has been murdered?"

"I'm not saying anything. Is there any reason why you would say that?"

"You just said that he was dead."

"But I never said anything about murder. Is there something that you want to tell me?"

"Not that I can think of at this moment. I was drinking with somebody; do you want him to come along as well?"

Floyd turned to the barman. "Is that true, was there somebody else in here."

"He's in the toilet."

Floyd told me to wait where I was and made his way through the door to the toilet. He was back in seconds. "There is nobody in there. Is there another way out?"

Steve, the barman, kept polishing his glasses as if murder was an everyday occurrence. "If you go down the corridor there is a fire door that leads to the car park at the side."

It looked like the information was too much for Floyd. "You coming peacefully, or do I have to cuff you?"

I drained my beer and put my trilby on. "Your car or mine, Sergeant?"

CHAPTER ELEVEN

As we walked into the car park, I could see that Detective-Sergeant Floyd was looking for any excuse to handcuff me. I went over to the Elf to lock her up, and he panicked, produced them from his pocket and rattled them in front of my face. I held my hands out in mock-surrender, and he put them back and escorted me closely to the front seat of the police car. There was a uniformed driver waiting with the engine running. Floyd sat behind so that he could keep an eye on me in case I wanted to throw myself out onto the road at high speed.

"Put the siren on, Dave. Foxley wants to see him urgently."

An idiot in the role of a policeman with a little bit of power can cause a lot of disturbance. As the siren screamed its message out into the Lake District darkness, and the big Ford Cortina picked up speed, the word 'overkill' sprang to mind. Obviously, the police around these parts didn't have much to do when it came to crime. Probably the biggest thing to happen in Woodley recently was a local cheating at dominoes. Having somebody murdered must be like getting a birthday and Christmas rolled into one. I sat back, relaxed, and looked forward to a fun evening unravelling in front of me. My biggest problem was trying not to laugh. I didn't to talk to Floyd anymore. If he did know something, which I doubted, he wasn't going to tell somebody like me. To rural police, private detectives were looked upon as something just a little lower on the evolutionary scale than rats.

Foxley had set up a temporary office in the kitchen and was questioning Vanessa Tate when we arrived. He looked up as we entered the room. "Ah yes, Mr Shannon. Nice of you to honour us again with your presence."

"He wasn't too happy to accompany me, sir." Detective-Sergeant Floyd had switched to full grovel mode. He was obviously trying to impress his boss.

"I always make a point of cooperating with the police," I said, "Especially if someone has been murdered."

"Murdered?" Vanessa Tate sprang to her feet with a shocked look on her face. Her jaw moved up and down in silence and liquid began to dribble from her eyes. "I understood that Mr Poole had died by accident."

"Well, miss, we are not sure yet what happened," said Foxley. "If you would like to sit down, maybe we can get a clearer picture. Floyd, can you go and rustle us all up a cup of tea."

If looks could kill, then I think me and Foxley would have been writhing on the floor in agony. Floyd pushed past me on his way to the door.

Foxley kicked a hardback wooden chair towards me. "Sit down, Mr Shannon; I'll come to you in a minute."

Vanessa was upset. "I was not aware that you thought Mr Poole had been murdered. You let me believe that the whole thing was a terrible accident." She sounded in need of a drink. She dabbed her eyes with a tissue and played nervously with a lock of hair.

"He's not any deader if he was murdered than if he died from natural causes. At this stage, we are keeping an open mind."

Her gaze wandered around the room and came to rest on me. I smiled sympathetically. "It's bad enough for me to have found the poor man dead, now I know that somebody killed him, I won't sleep a wink."

"Take it easy, miss. Let's just look at the events, before we jump to any conclusions. Now, talk me through it again. Why did you go into his drawing room at that exact moment?"

"I just popped my head around the door as I was passing, to see if he wanted a cup of tea. I had given him a lift to buy a takeaway from the village earlier on, and he always liked a cup of tea after one of those. He also had a habit of falling asleep after eating. Of course, I could smell the gas as soon as I looked in."

"So what did you do then?"

"It all seems like a blur. I rushed in and opened the window, and then I turned off the gas fire. I went over to Mr Poole. He was just lying there. At first, I thought he was asleep, but when I shook him, I knew...." her voice trailed off, and I expected more tears, but they never came. Underneath that fragile exterior, she was a tough cookie.

"So what did you do then?"

"I rushed out of the room and found Alfred. He came with me and called the ambulance."

"Can you tell me who was in the house at the time?"

"Well, there was Roxy, Lia, Alfred, and Sky." She thought about it some more and added. "And me of course."

Foxley flashed a reassuring smile. "I think maybe a good night sleep would be the best for you, Miss Tate. If you can remember anything else, then you know where to find me. Now, if you will excuse me, I need to talk to Mr Shannon."

"Yes of course, and thank you."

She left the room, still playing with her hair.

"Looks like bad things happen in the house every time you pay a visit, Mr Shannon." He stood up from his chair and crossed the room to where I was sitting. "I suppose you are going to put it down to coincidence."

"Why? What do you put it down to?"

"Why did you come back, Mr Shannon?"

"You need to talk to Roxanne Rothchester if you want to know that."

"I intend to. She is sedated just at the moment. Am I to believe that you are here officially, as an investigator?"

"Maybe she didn't like the way the police were investigating her husband's death and wanted to go private."

"There's no law against that. Did you see Sheldon Poole tonight?"

"No," I lied.

"But you saw Mrs Rothchester?"

"Roxy? Yeah, we spoke for about half an hour."

"About?"

"Like I said, you would need to talk to her. There is such a thing as client confidentiality."

"Is there? I thought that just extended to doctors and priests." He went back to his chair and scribbled something down in a notebook. "Did you ever talk to Sheldon Poole on your last visit?"

"Once or twice, but not what you would call an in-depth conversation."

"Did he seem to you the sort of person that would take his life?"

"How could I tell that? As far as I was concerned, he was just normal. Are you going to tell me what happened?"

"What happened, Mr Shannon is that he left to gas fire on without lighting it, went to sleep in a chair after eating a takeaway and died from the fumes. We are wondering if it was a defective gas fire, he did it on purpose, or it was a tragic accident."

"Or somebody walked in when he was asleep and turned it on without lighting it."

"You've got a suspicious mind, Shannon."

"I'm afraid that it comes with the job. Are you telling me that you have ruled out murder?"

"Are you making a confession?"

"What's my motive, Sherlock?"

"I'm sure I could think of something if I tried."

"Are you handling this as an accident or foul play?"

"Tragic accident for now, but after what happened to the husband I'm keeping my options open." He drummed his fingers on the table, and I tried to guess the tune that was in his head. "We will probably have a reconstruction tomorrow, but the trouble with detecting anything in that room is that everybody came running in before we arrived. They trampled on anything that could have been useful to forensics, though the team is in there now, trying to see if they can find something."

"My guitar gently weeps for you, Mr Foxley. Can I go?"

"One last question. When you were here earlier on, did you see any strangers around the place?"

I had been waiting for this question and asking myself how I was going to answer it. I told him about picking up Enrico Cicero, mainly to cover myself, as this could easily be checked. I left out the argument with Sheldon Poole until I had time to think it through. As it was, Foxley got excited at this small piece of information, especially when I told him that he had run out of the pub.

"Did he sound agitated when you picked him up?"

"He was a little bit drunk and in a fairly good mood. I'm not a psychiatrist and wasn't in an analytical disposition. Why don't you pick him up and see for yourself? Can I go now?"

"Yes. We know where you are staying, so expect to hear from me."

"I'll be looking forward to it."

I got a grudging police lift back to the Slaughtered Dog coutesy of Detective-Sergeant Floyd, and then made my way back to the hotel through the sleepy streets of Woodley. By the time I got there, I was dead on my feet. I let myself in to the darkened bar area, climbed up the stairs and fell into into bed. I was asleep before I had time to pour myself a nightcap.

CHAPTER TWELVE

"You took your time answering the phone."

"I was in bed."

"It's midday by my watch. I've been up since eight o'clock," I lied.

"Midday? I'm going back to bed. Ring me at a more reasonable hour."

"No, Shoddy, don't put the phone down on me. I've got some things that I need you to do." My partner, Shoddy was a night owl and also a raging alcoholic. The fact that he was my partner at all was only down to the fact that he had one of the sharpest brains of anybody I had ever met.

I heard him sigh. "What do you need?"

"Don't put on that tone of voice with me, Shod. You get half the money I get, so you need to do half the work."

This seemed to wake him up. Money always did. "I've got my pencil poised, Moggsy. Fire away."

I gave him a list of people that I wanted him to check and then asked him if he could use his police contacts to get me a crime scene report of Binky's murder. He complained a bit, but that was just the way Shoddy dealt with the world. Everything was too much trouble and just dealing with life on a daily basis was too complicated if it involved going anywhere other than the pub.

Shoddy was an ex-cop and a good one at that. Something went wrong on his climb to the top of the heap, and alcohol and drugs led to early retirement. That was bad luck for him, but good luck for me, as without him I wouldn't have the cheek to call myself a detective.

We had a fifty-fifty line drawn in the sand between us. He did all the intellectual digging, and I went out into the real world and got a daily dose of abuse and violence. We were the perfect team. Not exactly Holmes and Watson; more like Laurel and Hardy.

The caravan park was muddy, and the mobile homes were depressing and mostly in need of torching. There were about twenty of them on display, all with TV aerials and wrecks of cars parked in front.

There was a grey concrete building in the middle that showed the only sign of life. A red neon sign above the door flickered intermittently between SOCIAL CLUB and OCIA C UB. The neon looked out of place, and the words 'members only,' written in green biro underneath, filled me with pessimism. I pushed my way through the swing doors with an open mind. At the very least, I could get a drink.

I could hear the noise of a jukebox from the corridor. It was that record with the mad guitar work by Buddy Holly. As I entered the lounge, his tortured vocals pronounced his undying devotion to Peggy Sue, who apparently was pretty, pretty, pretty, pretty. I hated Rock and Roll almost as much as I hated caravans and camping. The combination of both on offer at that precise moment made me depressed. I needed a drink and was pleased to see that there was no queue at the bar.

I walked passed a table with a group of rough looking women drinking beer in pint glasses with what looked like rum and blackcurrant chasers. There were booths that lined three walls that were mostly empty, and a couple of middle-aged teddy boys in drainpipes and large blue suede shoes dancing near the old Wurlitzer, which looked as antique as the music coming out of it.

Summertime Blues came on, and a couple of the rum and blackcurrant ladies got up as well and joined in with the geriatric gyrating. It was showtime, though at this time of the day I couldn't get my head around the party atmosphere. Maybe it had something to do with living in a caravan or recreational drugs. I sniffed the air for signs of cannabis, but all I got was the stale smell of woodbines, body odour, and Virginia ready rubbed.

A big, brassy blonde in a shot silk chiffon blouse was pouring out generous measures of Polish Cherry Vodka for a couple of drunks on barstools. She had a chest that jiggled up and down like two giant soft-boiled duck eggs without their shells. When she had finished pouring, she came over. Up close, I could see the red puffiness around her jowls that had been semi- hidden by badly applied blusher.

"I'm Jade," she said with the faintest trace of a foreign accent. She gave me a blubbery-lipped genderless communal smile. "What can I get you?"

"Thanks, I'll have a beer and a whisky." Everybody else in the room was getting their rocks off by mixing their drinks badly, so why shouldn't I join them?

The only reason I had come to what must have been the equivalent of the wrong side of the tracks in Woodley, was because of something Enrico had said in the pub. I hoped the girl he had mentioned wasn't a figment of his vivid imagination. If she wasn't, then maybe he had come here after leaving me last night.

When she brought the drinks over, I told her to have one herself, and she poured out a gin and tonic. She smiled at me vacantly as she drank it, and sat down with a magazine.

Before she got settled, I asked, "Is Gilda here?" That wiped the look of contentment off her face.

"Are you a cop?"

"Do I look like one?"

She looked me up and down. "No, you look more like an insurance salesman. What are you selling, Luv?"

"Happiness."

"Keep some for me after you finished with her," she jerked a finger at a small girl sitting on her own in one of the booths, drinking a beer."

I walked over and sat down across from her without asking permission first. She didn't seem to mind. She looked over the rim of her glass. She had naive eyes that were the colour of every blue sky you'd ever seen. Not even the cheap makeup and gaudy red lipstick that had been plastered on her face could destroy its freshness. She examined me carefully, then went back to her drink and blanked me out with disinterest.

"I'm looking for Rico. Have you seen him recently?" I added, "I'm an old friend of his from the army."

She immediately became interested at the mention of the name. Maybe he hadn't been lying about everything. "You know Enrico?"

"We were best friends in the Falklands."

She lowered her voice so that it was barely discernible above the music. "I know how dangerous the work is that he does. Are you one of his friends from Special Branch? He's told me all about his undercover work."

"Maybe I am, maybe I'm not. I do need to speak to him urgently, Gilda. He gave me your name, and said I could trust you."

She bit her lip and got lipstick all over her front teeth, which I noticed were badly stained and crooked. "Rico is such a wonderful man."

I choked the words out. "Yeah, one of the best."

"And he told you I was one of the people you could trust?"

"Not one of the people, Gilda. The only person. Time is of the essence. Can I speak to him?"

"He might still be back at my place. He was still in bed when I left."

"Can we go and take a look?"

She drained her glass, and we walked back out onto the field. It didn't look any better after a drink. I followed her down what served as the main path between the vans until we came to a caravan under a tree at the far corner. The rest of the trailers looked deluxe compared to this one. I could see that the paintwork was blistered and peeling off, and the garbage near the door had an odour that screamed dead animal in the vicinity.

"So do you both live here?"

"No, he just visits me from time to time."

The door of the caravan was not locked and creaked when she opened it and went in. She turned on a lamp even though it wasn't that dark inside. "He's gone." She sounded disappointed.

"Are you coming in?"

"Thanks."

I climbed the two steps. The door was so low that I needed to duck my head to get in. The small space was grim even by my poor standards. There was a metal sink full of dishes and a calor gas stove that looked dodgy. At the far end was an unmade double bed covered in cheap blankets that looked like they needed washing. A table was cluttered with cups, plates, and cosmetics. The place made me feel like a giant who had stumbled into the bad fairy's cave.

"It's a bit small I'm afraid." She reached past me and closed the door. In the confined space, a combination of old grease, sex, cheap perfume and the smell of urine from the chemical toilet vied for prime position in the air.

"Nice place," I said.

"Would you care to sit down," she replied with dignity. "I don't have any beer, but there is some grappa if you like?"

"Thanks, but it's a bit early for me to hit the hard stuff."

I sat at the edge of the double bed with my trilby in my hand and wondered where all of this was leading to.

"If you're so anxious to see Rico, why not try his place?"

"I didn't know that he had a place."

"He doesn't often use it, especially when he is on a job. I've got the address here somewhere."

She opened up a drawer, and the contents sprang lose in an attempt to escape. She began to rummage through the turmoil. Finally, her hand emerged triumphantly holding a piece of paper like it was the Olympic Flame. "It's not that far from here, on the road to Workington. I've been there a couple of times. He lives on his own."

She dropped down beside me on the bed so that our legs were touching. This was too close for my liking.

I stood up, and she got up as well like my shadow. "Thanks again, Gilda, you've been a great help."

We were thrown together in the narrow aisle between the bed and the table. I tried to get past her and felt the touch of thighs and breasts as I attempted to leave with some dignity. She put her arms around my neck and was in the process of standing on her tiptoes to kiss me.

"How old are you, darling?"

She tried to pull my head down to hers, but I resisted. "Old enough and I need the money."

"I don't think seventeen is old enough. Why not go back to your family or get a proper job?"

She seemed to find this one highly amusing, and while she was laughing, I took her hands from my neck as gently as I could and made my way through the door. The cool air of the field tasted sweet, and I sucked it up hungrily like a man who had been drowning. She attempted to follow me out, but I blocked the way and handed her ten pounds. "Thanks for the information, Gilda; we always pay people who have been helpful." I touched my nose knowingly, and she seemed to understand.

Her face lit up, and she reached for my neck again, but I was too quick. She shouted after me. "Actually I'm eighteen, and it beats working in a factory. Now that you know where I live don't be a stranger, I treat my friends very well."

I shouted back that I wouldn't and that I was staying in the local pub if she needed to contact me. I realised it might have been a mistake to tell her that, as the words came out of my mouth, but I felt sorry for the girl. The images of Gilda sitting alone in her trailer, rattled around my head as I drove towards Workington. My brain was on fire with the thoughts of young girls similar to her, throwing their lives away before they had begun on men like Enrico Cicero and worse. By the time I saw the signs for Workington, I had come to the conclusion that I had no right to take the high moral ground, as I was probably throwing away my own.

CHAPTER THIRTEEN

I stopped at a mobile cafe at the side of the road just before I got to Workington. While I was eating a roast pork and stuffing roll with a mug of steamy tea, I looked at my map and tried to pinpoint Sandfield Terrace, which was the address I had written down. The closest that I could get to anything that sounded right was Sandfield Lane. I decide to head there in the hope that it led onto Sandfield Terrace.

The lay-by I had pulled into was full of trucks, and I was surrounded by an army of huge, ugly looking truckers that were taking a break. They cracked trucker type jokes to each other and looked at my suit, trilby and tailored coat with suspicion. I wanted to tell them that everything I had on was off-the-peg and probably didn't cost half as much as the Levis they were all wearing, but I stopped myself. They certainly bred them hard around this part of the world, and I avoided eye contact, finished a rather average snack, and continued my journey.

I found Sandfield Terrace, as I was hunting for Sandfield Lane. It sort of vaporised out of nowhere in the misty semi-darkness of a

Workington council estate. As an area, it made the word drab seem lavish. The street had houses spaced out between large patches of freeze-framed gloom, with the occasional speck of light thrown out from the cracks in badly aligned curtains. I counted just two working streetlights as I drove through the bleakness, and one of them flickered ominously like a disco strobe at a second rate night club.

I had been here for just two minutes, and the overwhelming icy touch of desperation made me want to go back to the warmth and security of the Rose and Crown. I felt like an old tomcat that was looking to get his tail torn off in a fight over somebody's discarded fish bone. Streets like this were my bread and butter, so I knew that I needed to put up or shut up. This was my environment, Shannon's world, which came with all of the dregs and low life scum I could handle. Unless I found myself other kind of work, this would be the sort of place I would be doing time in, until I eventually took my last breath and rolled face down in the gutter. On that happy thought, I got out to take a look around.

The rain was highlighted under the one working streetlight and streamed angrily down the dull beams onto my head and trickled off my trilby like a miniature waterfall. I was the only person out on a night like this, though I suspected that most nights were similar on Sandfield Terrace.

I was looking for number 12, and found it behind a strip of muddy grass and a broken and cracked concrete driveway. This place had a warped sense of reality, and number 12 looked abandoned except for the faintest glow from within. Unless I was mistaken, it was the glow of a TV or electric fire. I was pondering about the direct approach or the long, dull stakeout when the glow was extinguished, and a split second later, the door opened. A switch was triggered and threw out a yellow plank of light across the garden. A man's shadow appeared, and I made a dive back to my car.

After a while, I saw Enrico sauntering towards me, with the look of a man with not a care in the world. His car was parked just a few feet in front of mine. It was a Ford Escort. He walked past me as if I wasn't there, got in and drove away. I let him travel a few hundred yards before starting my engine and following from a distance with my lights off. I soon put them back on again after a couple of near misses and some angry drivers that questioned the relationship I had with my mother.

I followed him into the town centre, which was alive with the trickle of early evening rush hour traffic. Enrico was a nervous driver with an edge. He weaved in and out between the cars and took unnecessary risks. He was either in a hurry or knew he was being followed and making a half-hearted attempt at trying to get away.

We left the town behind and headed up the A596 towards Siddick and Maryport. This was the main road to Carlisle, and I hoped that he wasn't heading there because I didn't have enough petrol. We crossed a big river bridge and almost immediately, he swung his Escort into the car park of a large pub called The Old Admiral. I drove passed and turned around further up the road. By the time I got back to the pub, the Escort was parked near the door, and Enrico was gone.

The Old Admiral only had one large room, and it was gloomy and crowded. It was one of those old world fox hunting establishments that was full of polished brass and fading pictures of the landed gentry and their hound packs. Thankfully, the bar was discreetly lit and commanded a great view of the dining area, which was situated down a staircase on a lower split-level. It was just after eight o'clock and the place was doing great business. I ordered a beer and sat down in a corner near the wooden balcony that overlooked the tables. Enrico was sitting at one with his back to me. My luck was in. I had the perfect observation post with an endless supply of alcohol. My pessimism of the previous couple of hours, melted like a snowflake in a Finnish sauna, especially as I saw who was buying dinner. It was Binky's outspoken snob of a son Alfred and his strangely named wife, Sky.

It was after two o'clock by the time I made it back to the Rose and Crown. I had observed the conversation between the most unlikely threesome from a distance and hid in the toilet as Alfred paid the bill, and they left together.

By the time I got into the car park, there was no sign of Alfred and Sky, but I got a glimpse of the Escort with Enrico inside heading off down the road. He was probably going back to his house in the twilight zone. Apart from sitting outside all night until he woke up, there was nothing more that I could do.

I barely made it back to Woodley, and I was running on fumes and optimism by the time I arrived. That was another thing about being in the countryside. The petrol stations tended to shut at around Six o'clock in the evening.

As I lay in bed, my mind just wouldn't close down. It was seeing Alfred again that kept it and me awake. There was something that I couldn't put my finger on that went beyond his meeting with Enrico. Something that had happened on the night Binky was murdered that I had pushed to the back of my head as not important. It was an incident or a word that I had deemed as mere trivia at the time. A word, a phrase, an action? I couldn't lay my finger on it. Seeing Alfred and Enrico together had ignited a spark that refused to surface from my subconscious. I eventually drifted off into a troubled sleep.

CHAPTER FOURTEEN

"Did you get the police report? I put it in the post last night, Moggsy."

"It's upstairs in my bedroom, Shod. I just haven't opened it yet. You know I don't think straight before I've had breakfast. What about the rest of the people I told you to check out for me?" I was in the bar of the Rose and Crown in Woodley, speaking on the telephone to my partner Shoddy, and trying to stop Gwen, the landlady from listening in. She was hanging around my stool on the pretext of cleaning.

There was a pause on the other end of the line, and I heard Shoddy gulping something. I looked at my watch. It was ten o'clock, so I assumed it was alcohol.

"That man called Enrico Cicero is a strange one."

"You're telling me, Shod. What have you found out?"

"He was in the army for nine months before being dishonourably discharged for stealing. He spent three months in military prison before they kicked him out. He has also spent time in juvenile remand centres for the usual petty crime stuff."

"What strikes me as strange is how he got a job with a family like that, in the first place."

"It does seem a bit weird, Moggs, but listen to this. In the police report, there was mention of a huge insurance policy covering Binky's life. This was all linked to the roller coaster and fun park he was building. There is also a thing called, key-man insurance tied in."

"What's that?"

"Apparently, there was a company set up by the family, to build the pleasure park. Binky was the managing director, and the members of the board were his wife Roxanne, and his son Alfred. The company was called Rothchester Holdings. It's quite common to have this type of policy on the life of somebody who is considered important to the running of a business. The thing is the premium that they were paying out on the key insurance and the life insurance must have been colossal and financially crippling."

"So Roxy and Alfred will be getting a load of cash pretty soon. Are both policies with the same company?"

"Yeah, they are filed with a company called Standard Life. I guess that the company will want to make its own investigations, but if as you say, all of them had a perfect alibi, there is no reason that any of them can be suspected."

"Unless they paid somebody to do it."

"That's a possibility, but difficult to prove. Also, Capital Life would not get very good publicity not paying out on a policy that was taken out in good faith just for this type of thing happening."

"What? Murder you mean?"

"Well, not exactly murder, but the removal of Binky from the company. If the remaining family members don't get paid, they would more than likely win if they sued Capital Life, and it would be all over the newspapers. Don't forget, even though this family is on its arse, Binky still was a member of the House of Lords and a distant relative of the Queen."

"Really, Shod. How did you find that out?"

"It's called research, mate. You should try it sometime. When I say distant, it is very, very distant, but all the same..."

I understood what Shoddy meant. It was another world for the English Aristocracy, with or without money. He didn't have any more information to give me but said that he still had a few people to see. He told me that I should enjoy reading the police crime report and that it should give me at least one more lead to work on.

I ate a huge breakfast, washed it down with tea and walked upstairs to see what he had found out about Binky's death. It never failed to amaze me how Shoddy was able to access police information. He still had a load of friends in Croxley Police Station, but it seemed that this now extended to the Cumbrian Police as well.

The report made interesting reading. Binky had been shot in the throat with a .38 revolver while watching TV in his private sitting room. Nothing had been taken, but his body had been doused in pig's blood, and there was writing in pig's blood over the walls. On the wall behind the TV was written 'ban hunting.' And on the wall nearest the door, 'meat is murder.'

Detective Sergeant Floyd, who was the first to arrive at the scene of the murder, said that he had never seen so much blood and thought at first it had all come from the body. Later, a bucket with traces of pig's blood was found discarded in the garden. There were no fingerprints.

The report then went on to estimate the time of death, which was roughly when we had heard the shot. A thorough search had taken place for the murder weapon, which hadn't yet been found. In the conclusion section, a Mr Silvio Challinor, who was a local animal rights activist was named as a person that was of interest.

The pig's blood was a new angle, and so was the animal rights connection. Could Silvio Challinor be sending letters to Roxy because of the family involvement in hunting? Stranger things have happened, and people in the country had some weird ways of carrying on. I went down to the bar and looked up Challinor in the telephone directory. He was listed as living in Lower Woodley. I decided that he would be a good place to start the day's investigations.

It was just after one o'clock when I entered the sleepy little hamlet of Lower Woodley. It wasn't even attached to the main part of the village, and as far as I could make out didn't seem to be in a lower position. I assumed by the state of the houses that I passed that the lower in Lower Woodley referred to lower classes.

The buildings in this part of the region looked like surrealist symbols of yokel rebellion against the rich and powerful. Even the pub that I went passed looked more like a pub that you would see in the roughest part of Liverpool. This was obviously a place full of farm labourers and odd-job men. I concluded that the countryside· had to have its fair share of subservient employees to cater to the needs of the wealthy.

Number four Laurel Apartments occupied a three-story building next door to a junior school. It was painted a jaundiced yellow and looked as tired and worn out as the vehicles parked in front of it.

Inside the foyer, there was an old-fashioned cage lift with a sign saying out of order, and some concrete stairs, which I took. Number four was on the second floor, down a narrow veranda with panoramic views over a farmers market that had several stalls but not that many prospective customers.

The front window of number four was open, and inside there was a tired looking lady dropping uncooked French fries into a pan of hot fat that smelt old and well used. She was wearing a faded pink pair of dungarees with a woollen scarf around her neck. She was sucking an untipped cigarette that had a good half-inch of ash ready to fall into the chip-pan. She was either Silvio Challinor's mother, or he had a fetish for very old and extremely ugly women.

I coughed discreetly and wasn't heard over the sound of the chips screaming in the hot fat. I cleared my throat loudly, and she spun around and glared in my general direction.

"If you're looking for Sylvie, he's not here."

I put my head close to the window but was forced to back away because of the smell of the rancid corn oil and tobacco smoke. "Can you tell me where to find him?"

The ash fell off her cigarette onto a piece of sliced bread. She brushed it off, whilst maintaining eye contact. "Are you another one of those policemen?"

"No?"

"Insurance?"

"No."

"You're not the father of one of those women he hangs around with are you?"

"Absolutely not."

She came over to the window and leaned out. "You're out of luck. Sylvie went out a couple of hours ago, and won't be back until late."

"Do you know where I could catch up with him?"

"Know? I can see him from here. He's down there on the stalls. You can't miss him. He's got the one selling vegan products that no bugger wants to buy." She cackled like an old witch, lit up another cigarette and went back to the chip pan.

I thanked her and walked back down to the street. I crossed the road and meandered through the stalls. They were all selling meat at what looked like very reasonable prices. There was a van selling hot pork sandwiches and tea, and next to it, a stall full of farm produced cider that was luminous green. I was tempted to buy some for Shoddy, but it looked hallucinogenic. Next to this stall, there was a thin man with a shock of ginger hair, in jeans and an animal rights t-shirt. I used my honed-to- perfection powers of detection, to figure out who he was and walked over. The stall was a mishmash of products that smelt bad and looked like they could do your stomach serious damage.

"Mr Challinor?"

"Fuck off."

"I'm sorry?"

"You heard me, mate. You will be receiving the money for the stall rental shortly. It's in the post. Can't you guys from the council give a bloke some slack?"

"I'm not from the council, Mr Challinor."

"Are you a customer?"

"No."

"Then what do you want to talk to me for? If I owe you money, I ain't got it; if you are trying to sell me something, I don't want it, if I've made your daughter pregnant then prove it, or sod the fuck off."

"I'm a private detective looking into the murder of the Earl of Woodley and want to pick your brains."

"That's a new one on me. Don't you mean that you want to fit me up for doing the poor bugger in?"

"No, I mean what I just said. I'm interested in what your thoughts are about the pig's blood."

"All I've got to say is that I have been through this with the local police, and they obviously believed that I had nothing to do with it, or they would have arrested me."

"I'm willing to pay you for the information, Mr Challinor." I held up two ten pound notes.

"Call me Silvio," he said, putting on his coat and sticking a handwritten note on the counter saying 'back in five minutes.' "The pub's this way." He snatched the notes out of my hand and steered me past the food van. "I hope you realise that you're paying for the alcohol as well."

CHAPTER FIFTEEN

"It's not so much that I love foxes. It's just that I despise the people that chase after them on horses and still think that we live in the middle ages."

We were sitting in the bar of the local pub, called the Red Dragon, drinking bitter. It was one of the seediest places I had ever been in; infected with kitchen smells, stale beer and the stench of old men with horseshit on their shoes. This was a pub for farmers, and by the number of sheepdogs on display, this must have been their day off.

Challinor hadn't stopped talking since we had sat down with our beers, although for the life of me, I couldn't remember a word of what he had said. I tried to push the conversation around to murder.

"So what do you know about the murder of the Earl of Woodley?"

"Binky Rothchester? I've got my suspicions." He waved his empty pint glass in my face, and I took the hint and went to the bar.

"So what are these suspicions?" I asked sticking another glass of beer in front of him.

"Well, I didn't kill him for a start. I told the police that."

"This is not exactly a suspicion, Silvio. This is merely you denying that you did it."

"Yeah, but I reckons I knows who had a motive."

"Who?"

"Somebody who had an argument with Rothchester, and tried to pin the blame on me because he hates my guts."

"And his name would be?"

"That gob-shite Enrico Cicero. Do you know him? He works up at the Grange."

"Yes, I do know him, and he doesn't work there anymore because he was sacked."

"It couldn't have happened to a nicer person. That lad is not only a liar, but he's also got a nasty temper."

"Having a bad temper and being a liar doesn't make you a murderer, though."

"He's a womaniser."

"Neither does that."

"You can say what you want, mate, I think that he killed Old-Man-Rothchester and tried to make it look like I did it. That pig's blood trick was just for show."

"And did you tell the police?"

"Get real, will yeah. He used to be a mate. What do you think I am? A supergrass? I don't tell the police nothing."

"So what makes you so convinced that he killed him?"

"I saw them having a huge argument, and less than a week later Rothchester was dead."

"Where were they arguing?"

"In the grounds of Woodley Grange."

"What were you doing there?"

"I was in the woods."

"That's a strange place to spend your time."

"I was looking for traps. They paid Rico to do a lot of shit like that. One of his jobs was to snare rabbits for the pot. Those snares were inhuman, so me and a couple of mates used to go into the woods and deactivate them. I tell you, man, it was dangerous work, and finding one of those little fellas still alive screaming in agony at the pain of having its legs half cut off, made my blood boil."

"Do you know what they were arguing about?"

"Yeah, I stuck around long enough to get the gist. Rico was up to his old tricks and had been shagging Rothchester's daughter Lia. I tell you this; The Earl was well not amused. Those sorts of people don't like their bloodlines infected by commoners. I knew then that his days were numbered."

"How come?"

"Like I said; Enrico Cicero has a sadistic temper, and you don't argue with him."

"So why did he try to fit you up, with the blood thing?"

"Because I told him to stay away from my girlfriend, and he didn't like it, so he attacked me. He found out that I've got an even worse temper than him, and I knocked him out in front of a load of people in this very room. That hurt his pride. He was always boasting about being a tough as nails war hero, and couldn't take being laughed at by the villagers."

I finished my drink and got up to get two more in. "That's still not a reason to implicate you in a murder, though."

"Maybe not in your opinion because you are normal. Rico plays by a whole set of rules that only he understands. I reckon he must have been dropped on his head or something when he was a baby."

"Why do you say that?"

" Because I don't think that Rico has had a normal thought in his head since...well, since never. I tell you, the man is off his head. A total nutter."

CHAPTER SIXTEEN

By the time I left the Red Dragon with Silvio, he had become my number one buddy, and I was convinced that Cicero had killed both Binky and Sheldon Poole. He could have gone out of the back door of the kitchen, killed Binky and then returned. After we had heard the shot, it did take him a long time for him to come into the dining room after Roxy had called him. He was also near the house when Sheldon Poole was gassed.

As I staggered up the road to my car, Silvio was clinging onto my arm for support, and still spurting out verbal diarrhea about anything that came into his head.

When I left him steadying himself against a lamppost, he was trying to convince me that Elvis had been cursed by the squirrels that he had eaten. It was a theory that I didn't take that seriously, but I was certainly taking his observations about Cicero with more than a pinch of salt.

It was strange. He has an argument with Binky, and Binky winds up dead. I see him having an argument with Sheldon Poole, and Poole winds up dead. He falls-out with Silvio, and Silvia comes under suspicion of murder. I needed to pay him a visit and have a long chat.

Workington's version of the Bronx didn't look any better in daylight; in fact, it looked worse because you got to see the low-life walking about. Number 12 looked deserted as I walked up the path, but I knocked the door anyway, and a bleary-eyed Cicero answered after more than a minute.

It didn't register who I was for a couple of seconds, and then the colour drained from his face. Before he had a chance to recover, I had pushed open the door, and we were both eyeballing each other in the dilapidated hall, like two feisty stags ready to lock antlers.

"I don't know what your name is, mate, but you are trespassing on private property."

"So sue me, why don't you."

"Who are you?"

"I'm the bad tooth goblin, Cicero, and I'm prepared to knock a few of yours out if I don't get some answers."

"Answers about what? I ain't done nothing wrong."

"So you must have done something wrong."

"Eh?"

"It's a good job I'm not from the grammar police, Cicero, as I would be arresting you for the illegal use of a double negative."

He looked at me confused, and I took advantage and pushed him into what I assumed was the living room. He had been watching an afternoon film. It was Michael Caine in Zulu, one of my all time favourites. I wished I was settled at home in my flat in Croxley to watch it but switched it off all the same so that I wouldn't get distracted. I pushed him down on the settee and stood over him

"So tell me, why did you kill Binky Rothchester and Sheldon Poole?"

He looked up at me slyly. "I didn't kill either of them. That's just plain stupid talk."

"Funny how you had an argument with the two of them, and they both died."

"I'm not a killer."

"So why did you run away from the police the other night?"

"I've got my reasons, but I don't need to tell you. I'll ask you again. Who are you, mister?"

"Why did you have a meeting with, Alfred Rochester the other night?"

"Who says I did."

"I says you did, stupid. I was sitting in the pub watching you eat your meal."

"There's no law against eating, or have you just passed one. I don't know who you think you are, but I'll give you five to get out of my house. One..."

Before he had finished with number one, he jumped up, and head butted me on the nose, then leant back and kicked me between my legs. The pain from both parts of my body vied for position to see which hurt most. I could taste blood in my mouth, and a feeling of intense nausea was rising from my stomach. I grabbed hold of him and with all my strength launched him through the air. He hit the TV set and sent it tumbling over while he carried on and hit the wall. Like a scene from a Tom and Jerry cartoon, he slowly slid down it until he reached the floor. When he tried to get up, a heavy picture of a hunting scene burst free from its hooks and smacked him on top of his head, nearly knocking him out.

It nearly knocked him out but not quite. In seconds he was up and running at me again, screaming at the top of his voice. I hoped that he had understanding neighbours. I turned sideways and used his weight against him to hurtle his out of control body towards the door. The force of impact cracked the wood, and this time knocked Cicero out cold.

I used the opportunity to find a telephone and call the police. I asked if I could speak to DCI Foxley. I was told to hang on the line, and then that he wasn't in. I briefly mentioned it was to do with the murder at Woodley Grange, left Cicero's address with the person on desk duty. I told him to send a car around as a matter of urgency and then settled down to wait.

It was dark when Cicero eventually regained consciousness, and I realised that there was nobody coming. I told him to get his coat and that I was taking him to let the police sort it out. He told me that he was happy to go that he had nothing to hide and that he was going to file charges against me for assault.

I headed out towards the A596, and Cicero pulled the hood of his anorak over his eyes and feigned sleep. Traffic was sparse and became even sparser as we picked up the A595, towards Woodley. The road unrolled out in front of the Elf like black ticker tape under its wheels, and the grey rain clouds overhead seemed unsure about whether to move into full storm mode. The occasional streak of lightning illuminated the sky for the briefest of moments and the intermittent globules of rain played water sports on my windscreen and left me in turmoil about whether to use my wiper blades. I was the only vehicle on the road, and somebody seemed to have stolen all of the houses. It was like travelling through the desolation of the Gobi Desert, only without the sand and mosquitoes.

It was just after nine o'clock when the road took a nasty dip and plunged through a wooded area. Without warning, a large car shot across the road in front of us and stopped suddenly. I applied the brakes and braced myself ready to take the collision. The Elf span around and stalled, with the passenger side nearest the other vehicle.

Cicero had woken up, and had the door open and was out on the road before I had time to react. A figure stood in front of the mystery vehicle silhouetted against the headlights. They were on full beam, and I needed to cover my eyes to bring the scene into focus.

Cicero shouted sarcastically, "See you sucker," and walked slowly towards the figure. Those were the last words he would ever say. I saw the double-barrelled shotgun being raised almost lovingly, in slow motion. Cicero was oblivious to any danger until the first bullet ripped into his side and sent him spinning round like a tossed penny piece before hitting the floor hard.

This was my cue to react quickly, and I opened the driver's door and was hurtling towards the woods in a blind panic when a shot whistled over my head. I was hoping that whoever was doing the shooting, would now have to reload. I made the journey safely over the open ground and found the shelter of the woods. Underneath the trees, it was dark and relatively safe. I hid in the undergrowth and was just in time to see the silhouetted figure walk over to Cicero and empty both barrels into him before driving off.

I left it a good five minutes before emerging from the woods, and by this time, I could see the blue flashing lights in the distance. Just like the cavalry in a John Wayne Western, a battered old Rover, and a tiny Austin Metro rolled into town, a little too late to do anything about what had happened to Cicero.

DCI Foxley looked as if he could have done without the extra work. I sat in the back of the Rover, feeling sorry for myself and watching the arrival of the police doctor. It was none other than James Wellman; the boring pill-pusher I had spoken to briefly the night Binky was murdered. He walked past the car I was sitting in without acknowledging me even though I was certain that he had seen me.

Finally, the ambulance made a subdued entrance and loaded up the body. We drove off in a convoy just as the storm broke over the mountains, and the thunder and lightning turned the B movie into an

x-rated horror film.

CHAPTER SEVENTEEN

The officer behind the desk was talking down a microphone in a dreary monotone voice. "Car number P12, there has been an incident of domestic violence at number 15 Holly Avenue, Lower Woodley, can you let me know when you arrive."

He switched off the microphone, crushed out his Woodbine and lit up another.

I looked at him, and he smiled. "It's all go tonight. Won't be long now, sir."

"I hope so, sergeant. I've been sitting here for over an hour."

"These things take time, sir. I'm sure DCI Foxley will be calling for you in a minute or two."

"All this could have been prevented if you had not taken so long to send a car around."

The man behind the desk sighed. He must have been close to retirement and had met many people like me before in the course of his career. "We've been through this before, sir. Your call was logged in at just after five o'clock. The fact that it didn't get passed to the appropriate channel is a bit of a mystery, which I'm sure will be looked into. Unfortunately, other than this, I can't give you an answer."

Call me suspicious, but he didn't convince me.

I drifted in and out of sleep as I waited impatiently for Foxley to arrive. It was during one of these half lucid moments that I remembered what it was about the night Binky died that had been bugging me. It was so simple that I could have kicked myself for ignoring it. It was so outrageous that I needed to check it out before telling anybody and risk being laughed at. Proving my rather bizarre hypothesis was something that could be difficult, but I could work that one out later. At least my time asleep on the police bench hadn't been wasted. Shoddy had always rammed down my throat that if all of the believable clues didn't add up, then it was more than likely something that was unbelievable. I had to admit that if I was right, then it would take a lot to make people believe me.

Foxley arrived just as I had given up either way that he would be putting in an appearance. I followed like a pet dog into an interview room and sat down opposite him. His manner was cumbersome, with none of the friendliness he had shown me in previous meetings. He took my statement, passed it across the desk for me to sign, and then sat back in his chair. He was wearing the same suit that he had been wearing the first time we had met. I wondered if he had been home to get changed since that fateful night.

"It looks like we have found our murderer, Mr Shannon. Do you agree?"

"It seems likely, but I wonder who killed Cicero."

"Fortunately for you, this is something that you don't need to get involved in. The sleepy village of Woodley hasn't been the same since you arrived. What is it? A couple of days in total, and three bodies."

"Are you saying that I cause the murders, Mr Foxley?"

"I'm not saying anything, lad. Mine is not to reason why. My task is to clean up everything afterward. My advice to you is to quit while you are still breathing, and disappear to wherever you came from."

"Are you running me out of town, Mr Foxley?"

"Why, have you grown fond of the place?"

"It does have a certain charm."

"Let me talk very plainly to you, Shannon. We have solved two murders, and now, before I get home to my wife and children, I am going to have to attempt to solve another one. I could do without the complication of you turning up at the scene of any more dead bodies." He put my statement into a folder and got up. "Take my advice, and get the hell out of here. Leave it to the professionals."

With that, he walked out.

I found my car in the car park in front of the police station. I looked at my watch. It was nine a.m. I had been sitting on the bench for most of the evening. Even though it was early morning and I wanted to go to bed, there was one more visit I needed to make before I hit-the-sack. I started the car and head in the direction of Woodley village centre, and Dr Wellman's surgery. I didn't have a clue where it was, but it took me just one stop to ask in the local newsagents to find out the address.

The door to the surgery was up a small alleyway and open. The sign in the hall as I went in advised me that the hours of opening were 8:30 am until 10:30 am. There was a flight of stairs that led up to a waiting room that was empty, and at the far end of the room, was a door with a sign on it saying, Doctor. It was ajar.

I waited for about five minutes just in case there was a patient in there with him. Nobody came out, so I went near to the door and listened. It was silence except for a large grandfather clock ticking in the corner. I put my head around the door and looked in.

I only needed a couple of seconds to realise that the doctor was dead. He was lying at the side of his desk staring empty-eyed up at the ceiling. He had a big red stain covering his white shirt. I walked over and like an idiot felt for a pulse, which I knew was not going to be there.

As a decision, it didn't take much thinking about. There was nothing that I could do for Doctor Wellman, and I didn't want to spend any more time sitting on a police bench waiting for DCI Foxley to deliver another sarcastic speech about my presence in the village and the growing number of corpses. I let myself quietly out,

making sure not to touch anything.

CHAPTER EIGHTEEN

In the growing darkness of early evening, I pulled up outside Woodley Grange, refreshed after several hours of sleep back at the Rose and Crown. The news about Cicero and Dr Wellman being shot had spread around the village like an out of control bushfire. Gwen, the landlady of the pub, had stood over me while I was eating a late breakfast and gave me the full story, which was circulating around the locals. This amounted to nothing concrete, as not even the police had a good idea of who the perpetrator was. Her conclusion was that it was due to too much violence on TV and too many foreigners coming into the area. The way she was looking at me, I wasn't too sure if she included me in her broad definition of what a foreigner was. I guess to her; it was anybody born outside of Woodley.

She didn't seem to get the joke, when on my way out; I told her that I would let her know if I saw any Latin looking gentlemen wearing dark glasses and carrying violin cases wandering around the High Street. Still, at least the murders had given the good people of the village something interesting to talk about.

There was a kind of emptiness about the Grange as I rang the bell. There were no lights visible. I tried the handle, but it was locked. I rang the bell a second time, and after a while, somebody turned on the hall light, and the door opened slowly. It was Vanessa Tate. Her eyes were puffy as if she had been crying, and she peered into my face as if she had never seen me before. "Oh, it's you." She didn't sound that overjoyed for me to be there.

"I'm sorry to disturb you, but would it be possible to speak to Roxy?"

"She's having an afternoon nap. I suppose you know what has happened, to Doctor Wellman?"

"Yes, it's a terrible thing. This has something to do with what I wanted to see her about. Could you see if she is awake?"

"I'm not sure if that would be a good idea. She took the doctor's death very hard."

"I wouldn't have come if it wasn't urgent, Vanessa. Could you do this for me?"

She thought about it for a moment and then moved to one side. "Very well, you had better come in, and I will see what I can do."

She left me waiting in the room where Sheldon Poole had been gassed to death and disappeared. When she came back, her face had turned white with anxiety. "Her door is secured from the inside, and she doesn't answer when I call."

I took her arm and moved her out into the hall. "Do you have a spare key?"

"It's not a key; it's an iron bolt. She has never used it in all of the years I have worked here."

"Show me," I said.

She almost sprinted back up the stairs and led me through several corridors until we came to a solid looking heavy oak panelled door. Vanessa cried out "Roxy, are you OK?" and I put my shoulder against the panels. It was solidly constructed and didn't budge an inch.

"Are you certain that she is in there?"

"I am certain. I took her some tea and biscuits up a couple of hours ago. She was writing at her desk."

"I'm going to have to break in." I put my head against the wood and listened for a sound within. There was nothing, but I could see that there was a light on, when I put my eye against the keyhole. All that I could make out on the inside were the curtains drawn across the window.

I ran at the door and had the satisfaction of it giving slightly. Maybe the oak panels weren't that solid after all. Unfortunately, for me, my shoulder wasn't that solid either, so it took me several well-aimed kicks to break through. The wood tore, and the door flew open.

There was a huge wardrobe with mirrors on the front that took up most of one wall. To my left, there was a king size bed that had not been slept in. Roxy was lying face down on an antique writing desk her head turned to one side, resting on her forearm.

I knelt beside her and felt for a pulse. She was dead.

Vanessa was whimpering softly in the doorframe, and another figure appeared behind her. It was Lia. She pushed passed Vanessa and stood in the middle of the room looking at her mother, with no outward sign of emotion. This was aristocratic stiff upper lip gone mad. Her eyes were moist and accusing but nothing more.

"What's going on? Why are you here?"

"Your mother is dead, Lia. Vanessa, can you take her downstairs, then go and phone the police."

She turned away, and Vanessa put an arm around her sagging shoulders and led her away, sobbing gently. I closed the door behind them and went back over to where Roxy lay. I checked the windows. They were shut and locked. Nobody could have entered the room or left it. I returned to the desk and saw the bottle of valium on its side. It was empty.

Under her arm was a white sheet of paper with some writing on it. I very carefully eased it up a little bit with a pencil so that I could read it.

I am sorry to have to take the easy way out, but it seems that everything I have ever loved has been taken away from me. I'm feeling sleepy already, and I don't think that I can write anymore.

Please forgive me for being a coward, but

That was it. Apart from the letter, and the empty bottle f sleeping pills, there was nothing else on the desktop, but there was a drawer at the front that I could just about open without disturbing Roxy's lifeless body.

I used a tissue to cover my fingers to do a quick search. It was mostly filled with pens, pencils, paperclips and bills. There was a chequebook that showed she had £100 in her current account with Barclays Bank and some lose change. Stuffed right at the back, I found a personal letter that was handwritten on a single sheet of blue paper with the letterhead of the Shipton Hotel in Cockermouth.

Hi Roxy,

It's been so long, and I know that you and Binky are very busy with your new project, but what about coming up to stay with Giles and me for the weekend. We are not that full at the moment so I can

offer you the best room in the hotel (half-price – Joking!)

We could take in a theatre show, and you could try out our new

spa. We have an absolutely divine Vietnamese girl who does

unbelievable massages with hot stones.

Did I tell you that we are thinking of buying the property next

door and knocking through? Giles is thinking of installing a steam

room and gymnasium. You really must come over, darling. It must be

terribly boring for you to be stuck in that dreary old home of yours.

We've got at least six months news to catch up on. Give me a call.

I'm sure Binky can survive a few days without you, And so can you-

know-who!!!!

Love to you all. Ring me!

Lulu xxx

There was no date on the letter. I wondered how far Cockermouth

was and what the reference to you-know-who meant. I made a note

of the address and had just put everything back into the drawer when

I heard to sound of heavy footsteps approaching down the corridor. The door opened, and DCI Foxley came into the room. When he saw me, he grimaced and shook his head.

"What is it with you and dead bodies, Shannon?"

"I didn't kill her Mr Foxley; I am merely in the wrong place at the wrong time."

He went over and took the pulse of Roxy, before turning his attention back to me. "I was rather surprised that you weren't present this morning when we discovered Dr Wellman in his surgery. Still, you've made up for it now." He picked up the suicide note, read it and placed it back on the desk. "You knew the lady a bit. Any ideas why she would kill herself?"

"Apart from her father and husband being murdered in the space of a couple of weeks, and a close friend being shot today. No. Nothing springs to mind. Oh yeah, and let's not forget Enrico Cicero. I guess you would not have called them close, but there is a connection there."

He walked over to the window and checked it as I had done. "I was told that the door was locked from the inside. Is that true?"

"It was bolted, and the windows have anti- burglar locks on them, so I think we can safely say that this was suicide and not murder."

He looked around the room. "Unless there is some secret passage in here. With these old houses, you never know."

"Well, yes, there is that, but I suppose you would be able to find out by testing the walls."

Foxley sighed deeply. "Yes, but I suppose it's stretching the imagination. Like something out of an Agatha Christie novel."

"Or Ngaio Marsh," I quipped.

"Who's he?"

"It's a she actually. Sort of an alternative to Christie, if you like that sort of thing."

"I'm afraid I prefer romantic comedies, Shannon." He looked at me hard with a frown on his face.

"I told you this morning to go home and leave all this to the professionals. That was a friendly warning, but this time it is official. Go back to where you came from Shannon."

"So you are running me out of town."

"I am asking you to leave. I am also saying that if you don't, I might start to think you have something to do with all this. Following on from that logic, I could arrest you and hold you for questioning. I could make life very difficult for you. Wouldn't it be better if you just went home and found another client to give you a case to resolve?" He opened the door, and without looking at me said. "Good day, Mr Shannon."

"But...what.?"

"I said good day, Mr Shannon."

"Don't you want...?"

"Morris Shannon, I am arresting you on suspi...."

"Ok, I'm going." I headed through the door and found my way back to the car park. I checked my map and estimated that

Cockermouth was about a forty-minute drive away. I didn't have much to go on but maybe a talk with Roxy's friend, Lulu, would throw some light onto the weird sequence of events that were happening in Woodley.

CHAPTER NINETEEN

The lady behind the reception desk of the Shipton Hotel was either French or Italian. She examined my crumpled suit and battered trilby as if I had no right to have walked into the place. She was probably right. This was a five-star hotel, and the guests that stayed here looked down on the likes of people such as me. She looked relieved when I mentioned Lulu's name.

As if to confirm it she said, "Who was it that you wanted to see?"

Unfortunately, I didn't have her second name. "Lulu,' I repeated. " She is the owner."

"One moment please." She picked up the telephone and talked into it. She looked me up and down as she was speaking then examined me with question mark eyebrows. "Mrs Lucinda Huffly-Green would like to know who you are."

Now that was a name and half. "My name is Morris Shannon. Tell her that I'm a friend of Roxy Poole."

After a brief conversation, she put the phone down, and I got a radiant smile. "Mrs Huffly-Green will be down shortly. Can I get you some tea?"

I thanked her for her kindness but said no and sat down on a luxurious sofa near a crackling log fire. It was times like these that I loved my job.

A very tall woman appeared like a genie through a door I hadn't noticed. She had executive permed blonde hair and worldly hazel eyes that told a story I would never have enough money to hear. She glided towards me, and I instinctively got up like a gentleman to greet her. I imagined that the body underneath the elegant clothing had spent many hours in the gym or under the critical eyes of a personal trainer.

She gave me a firm business handshake and sat down on the settee next to the cushion I had just risen from. She obviously wasn't a firm believer in creating a personal space for herself. This showed the mark of a confident tactile businesswoman.

She didn't waste time on niceties. "What's this all about, Mr Shannon?"

"I'm a private detective, and until today I was working for your friend Roxanne Poole."

The alabaster smile on her face wavered. "And now?"

"Like I said, I was working for your friend on a case that was very delicate. You know of course about what has happened recently at Woodley Grange?"

"Yes, of course I know. It has all been very tragic, especially the accident to her father. I spoke to Roxy only the other day, and she never mentioned that she had hired a private detective. It seems very cloak and dagger. Still, Roxy is always one for going private, and I suppose the police in Woodley are not up to that much. So does Roxy have a problem? Is that why you are here?"

"I'm afraid that your friend committed suicide this afternoon. She's dead."

"You are kidding."

"It's not the kind of thing that I would kid you about."

"But why?" She was keeping relatively calm, but a few tears started to roll down her cheeks.

"She has had a difficult time lately, and that's why I'm here. I was hoping that you might be able to throw some light onto why she managed to get depressed enough to take her own life."

She took out a petite lace handkerchief from her pocket and dabbed her eyes. The droplets were already eroding her makeup. She delved into her handbag and brought out a lipstick, which she applied automatically. While she was doing this, I explained the series of events leading up to my visit to Woodley Grange and finding Roxy's body. She didn't interrupt until I mentioned Dr Wellman.

"You knew that they were lovers, I assume."

Now that was a revelation. Bubbly, extrovert Roxy and the boring doctor! That was just too bizarre for words. "No, I didn't know that."

"So what were you investigating, Mr Shannon?"

"Roxy had received some threats through the post. She hired me to find out who it was."

"And who was it?"

"I don't know."

"So you have come to me to see if I can help."

"Yes."

"It could have been anybody."

"Yes, but in cases like these, it is usually somebody that the victim knows. Do you know of anything that Roxy had done to bring this on herself?"

She called for a pot of coffee and sat back. "Roxy and I go back to boarding school. We were best of friends then, and we have always tried to maintain links with each other. She seems to be a happy-go-lucky sort of a person on the outside, but I can tell you that she has had a tragic life. When we were in university together, we were in a click of people, and she fell in love with a student who was studying medicine. His name was..."

"James Wellman," I interrupted.

"Exactly. Believe it or not, in those days, James was such a funny guy. I believe that what happened turned him and left him bitter and more than a little bit empty."

"So you are saying that Roxy ran off with Binky and that broke his heart?"

"Not exactly, though Binky was part of our crowd at Oxford. We were all born in and around Woodley. Other students used to call us the Woodley Set. You have to understand that Roxy was a wild one in those days. She got pregnant, and James refused to accept the baby."

"Then surely he has only got himself to blame."

"Not really, Mr Shannon. Roxy committed two crimes. Firstly, she got pregnant by another man. And secondly, she admitted it to James. He was so hurt that he dropped out of Oxford and finished his medical training in Canada."

"So who was the father?"

"Only Roxy knew that, and she wasn't telling. I had my suspicions, but they were just that."

"Binky?"

"Good God, no. Roxy had never even looked at Binky in that way until..." The coffee arrived, and she poured it out, sat back and lit a cigarette. I waited impatiently for her to continue.

"Until what?"

"Until she had lost James and didn't know what to do. She seduced Binky, told him that she was pregnant and that he was the father. He did the right thing and married her. Binky never was the brightest lamp in the street. The fact that Lia was born very early didn't seem to click in his brain."

"So you think that he never suspected?"

"I think that if he did, then he wasn't bothered. Let's face it. Even though he was a Lord, somebody like Binky would have had no chance of catching a person like Roxy. It was a marriage of convenience. Roxy needed a father for her child and a title. I think

Binky was just happy that she agreed to marry him, though I might be wrong. Binky could have just been stupid."

"So how come the affair between Roxy and James started again."

"By chance. James's father died and left him the house in Woodley. He moved there and just sort of drifted back into the relationship with Roxy. Binky didn't have the faintest idea. That's for sure."

"Did she ever get depressed?"

"No. She was a very positive person."

"Did you know that James Wellman was murdered this morning?"

"No, but I think that provides you with the reason why Roxy did what she did. Who killed James?"

"I have no idea, but as you say, that is the perfect motive for Roxy to commit suicide."

She got up quickly. "I really must give Lia a call. What must that poor girl be going through?"

I stood up as well. "Sorry to be the messenger of such bad news."

"I'm glad you did. It has probably been all over the radio and local news, but running a hotel, you don't have time to listen or read anything."

"What will you do now?"

"I'm not sure at the moment."

She gave me her hand again. "Goodbye, Mr Shannon, and thank you."

The moon was high in a cloudless sky as I drove back to Woodley. The events of the day had produced another two bodies and muddied the already dirty water that surrounded the events of the last few weeks.

I stopped at a payphone on the way back and spoke to Shoddy. I had another one of my hunches that I wanted him to confirm before I put the lid on the case and went home. I also phoned up Cynthia, who was the reason I had been dropped into the mess in the first place. The two simple questions that I asked her didn't leave me any closer to the truth, but gave me a reason, at least, to pay one last visit

to Woodley Grange.

CHAPTER TWENTY

I didn't set my alarm, so I slept in until after midday. It would have been longer if the telephone hadn't woke me up. It was the landlady.

"Mr Shannon, there is somebody here that wants to see you. She's been here for a while; you haven't been answering your phone."

"I was asleep," I said defensively.

"Of course you were. Shall I prepare your breakfast?"

"Just a couple of soft boiled eggs and some coffee, please. Tell whoever it is that I will be there in a minute."

I had a quick shower, cleaned my teeth and got dressed.

When I walked into the empty bar, I didn't see her at first. She was sitting huddled up by the log fire staring into the flames as they slowly devoured the wood. The slightly damp logs were throwing out white smoke and a heavy pungent smell, which combined with the scent of old beer. This was the typical opening time smell of a traditional pub. I loved this aroma; it made me feel at home and in need of a proper drink. I resisted the temptation and just made do with coffee and eggs, which the landlady brought through as I approached the table where Gilda was sitting. She declined an offer to join me for breakfast, and I knocked the tops off my eggs and settled down to listen. She had obviously got a story and looked like she had been up all night perfecting the details.

"I'm sorry to come here, but you did say I could."

"No problem, are you sure that you don't want some coffee? You look as if you need it." She was wearing a black Parka with a furry hood and more zips than I could count. Her jeans looked like they needed washing and the white stiletto boots looked distinctively out of place in the overall vibe.

"It's just that I didn't know who to turn to."

I put on my most reassuring voice. "No, really. You did the right thing. Now, what's happened?"

"It's all over the news that Rico has been shot."

"Yes, I know. It was a terrible thing."

"He was a wonderful man, Mr Shannon."

"Yes wonderful." I nearly choked on one of my toast soldiers, which I had just dipped into a large brown egg."

"Can I trust you, Mr Shannon?"

Not another one! "Of course you can, darling, but I need to know what the problem is. Are you just upset?"

"No, well, yes; I am upset, but that's not the reason I'm here. I heard the news about Rico when I was in the club, and I knew that there was going to be trouble for me."

"How could you know that?"

"Because Rico told me the last time I saw him that there might be some trouble, but if he was lucky, then he would be making a lot of money, and we could go away together."

It sounded like the typical line that Enrico Cicero would spin to a woman. Especially one as gullible as Gilda. "So did he tell you what kind of trouble?"

"No, but he gave me two packages to keep safe for him. He told me to take good care of them because they were worth a lot of money."

"What was in the packages?"

"I haven't looked."

"Where are they?"

"I'm not sure if I can tell you. Rico told me not to trust anybody."

"Well, with all due respect, Gilda, what are you doing here then?"

She started to cry. I hate it when women cry in front of me. I never know what to do. I poured myself a second cup of coffee and waited for her to calm down.

Eventually, she stopped. "I knew that there was something wrong when I walked back from the club. The door of the caravan was wide open, and the place had been ransacked. That was it for me. I just ran out of there, and have been walking around the village all night."

"Perhaps you should go to the police. Do you want me to take you?"

"I don't want to have anything to do with the police. Rico said that those packages were worth a lot of money. It's sad that he's gone, but now I have to look after number one, and that's me. I could be set up for life, and I don't intend to throw my chance away."

I realised then that Gilda wasn't crying for Enrico she was crying for herself. She was afraid after what had happened to her caravan. "So how can I help?"

"I need to get away from here. I've got a sister in Plymouth. I could go and stay with her and take it from there."

"So I repeat, what do you want me to do?"

"There is a train tonight at ten o'clock. Can you look after me until then? I can pay you." She unzipped one of her pockets and took out a five-pound note and some loose change and held it out to me."

"That's OK, Gilda. You can pay me back when you are rich. Don't you need the money for the train fare?"

She tapped another one of the zips. "No that's all sorted out."

"You can stay with me until then, and I will run you to the station and put you on the train personally. How's that?"

I got a smile for the first time. She leaned over and rubbed the top of my leg like I was a cocker spaniel who had just performed a trick. "I think that I can trust you, Mr Shannon."

I poured us both a cup of coffee and relaxed back in my chair. She thought that she could trust me to look after her, but not enough to show me what Cicero thought could make him big money. I looked at my watch. It was coming up to half past two. Time to go and pay a visit to Woodley Grange. If I was lucky, this would be the last time.

CHAPTER TWENTY-ONE

I left Gilda sitting in the front of the Elf reading the Daily Mirror with the doors locked. I wanted her to stay in the pub and barricade herself in my room, but she insisted on coming with me, saying that she felt safer knowing I was close. I told her to give a blast on the horn if she needed me. I remembered as I rang the doorbell that the horn on the Elf hadn't worked for a couple of weeks. I thought about going back to tell her but decided against it. If I did that, she might insist on coming in with me, and that would not be a good idea.

Alfred's wife Sky answered the door and didn't look particularly pleased to see me. I asked if I could speak to Lia, and she ushered me down yet more dilapidated and winding corridors to a room that said office on the door.

It was a very business -like room that looked like something out of a novel by Charles Dickens. I would not have been surprised to see Ebenezer Scrooge writing with a quill pen into a dusty old ledger. Instead, I got Lia and Vanessa Tate, drinking tea off a silver tray and sitting on a huge Victorian settee.

Vanessa Tate moved her gaze from choosing what type of biscuit she wanted and turned it on me.

"Here again, Mr Shannon. I rather thought that we had seen the last of you."

Sky left the room, and I stood by the door clutching my trilby for comfort. This was a very intimate scene between the two women, which I felt I was violating. Now, both their heads were turned towards me, willing me to leave.

"I hope that you are recovering, Lia." As soon as the words came out of my mouth, I regretted them as pretty dumb.

"I haven't been ill, Mr Shannon. I have merely lost my mother, father, and grandfather in the course of a few weeks. I don't think any antibiotics will get me through this one."

"No of course. What I meant to say was..."

Vanessa interrupted me. She patted Lia's hand protectively. "Yes, I'm sure we are both aware of what you meant to say, Mr Shannon. Now, can you please get on with the reason why you are here? You are not the real police, and I am quite certain they are quite capable of doing their job without your interference."

"I'm not sure if you know, Lia that your mother hired me because she was getting threatening letters and she didn't want to go to the police about them?"

"So are you insinuating that the family owes you money, Mr Shannon?" asked Vanessa.

"No, I was paid before I started the job. It's just I like to finish anything that I investigate. Do either of you know anybody that could have sent her the letters. Did she confide in either of you?"

They both shook their heads. Lia glared at me as if I had made the whole thing up. "Have you got any of these letters?"

"No."

"Then why should we believe anything that you say?"

"Because why should I lie?"

Lia laughed hollowly at this. "Could it be that you want us to pay you to carry on with your sordid investigation. It's just your word. Unfortunately, mother can't back you up, can she?"

"I repeat, why lie about a thing like that? That would be monstrous."

"Exactly," said Vanessa. "That's why I think that this conversation is a little bit distasteful. If you have anything to say, then say it to the police. Ever since you have arrived here, there has been nothing but trouble. I think that you should go home, Mr Shannon. And leave us to grieve in peace."

It was totally illogical what she had just said, but what could I say? In the end, I decided to say nothing and just leave. I'd been paid, my client was now dead, and so there was no reason to hang around.

I walked through the labyrinth of corridors alone, thinking what Roxy would have made of what Vanessa and Lia had just said. The corridors were cold and empty, and I had the distinct impression that I was going in the wrong direction. People that lived in small houses like me didn't understand the complexities that owning a large house can give you. Being able to get to the front door was one of them.

There were ley lines of violence and depression running through Woodley Grange that were in a permanent state of chaos. They ebbed and flowed like a furious ocean. I couldn't wait to get out of the place and head for home; having first made a detour to the station with Gilda. It was just as I came to an old staircase and realised that I had never seen it before that the lights went out.

I was in total darkness, like being inside a coffin. The floorboards creaked suggestively behind me.

"Hello," I shouted. There was no reply, but the floorboards creaked again. There was somebody walking down the corridor that didn't want me to know that they were there. I shouted "Hello" again. I needed a weapon, but I couldn't even see my hand in front of my face let alone be able to search for such a thing. I flew up the stairs as fast as I could, grateful that whoever it was in the corridor below was experiencing the same total blackness as me. I reached the landing on the floor above and began feeling my way down the wall. I could hear the stairs groaning behind me. Somebody was coming up fast. I found a door handle and tried it, but it was locked. Was I being herded like an animal, or was it just my imagination. At the end of this corridor, there was a spiral iron staircase that descended into the bowels of the house. I made my way down, carefully. There was a door at the bottom, and I opened it and went through. I almost lost my legs, as I didn't see the steps going down. I grabbed hold of a wooden banister to steady myself.

This wasn't a corridor but a large room. I felt the wall. It was bare stone and was damp and dripping with condensation. I stayed very still against the wall and waited. In this darkness, I wasn't going anywhere, so my best chance was to hide in the shadows and let whoever it was go past.

I heard the sound of feet running down the stairs, and I pushed myself further back onto the wall. I heard footsteps coming down the stone steps and moving towards me across the wooden floorboards. Coming out of the darkness, the figure of a man appeared. I couldn't see who he was because he was wearing night vision goggles that covered half of his face. He stared straight at me. He had a gun in his hand, which he raised.

I kicked out at him and missed, then turned to run away. As I did so, something heavy crashed down on the back of my head, and I lost consciousness.

CHAPTER TWENTY-TWO

I was dancing around my flat in Croxley with Roxy, and she was in a black bra and panties. Binky burst into the room and shouted that he had caught me trying to seduce his wife. I tried to tell him that I was an erotic ladies underwear salesman and I was trying to sell her some, but he didn't seem to believe me. Suddenly he wasn't Binky at all, but he had morphed into his son Alfred, who kept shouting, "You're nothing but an erotic ladies underwear salesman."

Somewhere during his torrent of abuse, I opened my eyes and felt the blood pumping between my ears like heavy surf on a deserted shingle beach. I tried to raise my head a little, but a lightning flash of pain burst into flames in my eyeballs. I stared up at the ceiling. It had thick wooden oak beams with meat hooks dangling from them. I lay very still for a while, feeling the sweat against the surface of my skin and listening to the rumble of drums play conga rhythms in my brain.

At least I was still alive. I wondered why. I remembered that I had left Gilda sitting in the car. Would she come and look for me or drive off. There was a dim yellow light in the room that came from a bulb located behind wire meshing on one of the walls. I stood up and rubbed my forehead.

"You're awake. Thank God. I thought you were dead, but I was too scared to check."

I turned around. It was Gilda. She was sitting on a wooden stool near an old kitchen table. The place we were in looked like an old deposit, where they probably would have hung meat in the olden days. She was still wearing her black parka, and she looked as if she had been crying.

"How long have I been lying here?"

"About an hour. They tried to wake you up and got very angry when you wouldn't."

"Who are they?"

"I've seen them before, but I don't know their names. The woman has a face like a mule."

That must be Alfred and Sky. "How come you are here?"

"It was the lady. She came out when I was sitting in the car and asked me if I wanted to come in and wait. She said you had asked her if I could."

"I did nothing of the sort."

"Yeah, I know that now, but at the time she seemed so friendly. It was when I got out of the car, and the man appeared that things got out of hand. He told me that he knew I was Rico's girlfriend and that I had some things that belonged to him that Rico had stolen."

"So how did he know that you were Rico's girlfriend?"

"Because I did some cleaning here a couple of times and Rico got me the job. I'd seen them both around the place, but why would I be interested in who they were?"

"So what happened?"

"He said that unless I gave him what he wanted, I was going to end up the same as Rico."

"So you told him where the packages where?"

"Well, not exactly."

"What do you mean not exactly?"

"Well, I sort of told them that I had given them to you and you had hidden them somewhere safe."

"What? You told them that I had the packages?"

"No hidden them."

"Yeah, that makes a difference." I shook my head in disbelief.

"Don't be angry. They would have hurt me if I hadn't told them something."

"Yes, but they are still going to hurt you, and me as well if we don't think of something fast."

She went into her pocket and brought out a letter. "This is one of the packages that they were looking for."

"It's not a package. It's a letter."

"Yeah, well I never was very good at explaining things. I haven't read it. Do you think it could be important?"

I walked over and took it out of her hand. "Let me have a look, and I'll tell you."

The envelope was postmarked Woodley and dated the day that Binky had died. It was addressed to his daughter, Lia so that she would have probably got it the next day. I opened it.

My darling little girl,

I don't know how to start this letter except by telling you how much I love you, and that I always will. You have always been a joy to me, and I can think of nobody else in the world that has brought me more happiness.

Lia, there are times in life where things get so bad that you can't think of anywhere to turn. I have had many times like this but have always pulled through knowing that there is a light at the end of the tunnel. This time, however, I can see no way out.

I discovered that your mother is having an affair with Dr Wellman. When I confronted them, they laughed and told me that they had been lovers since we were at Oxford together and that I had always been a fool.

I spoke to your grandfather about it, and as far as I can see, he was part of the subterfuge against me. I have been living a lie for all these years. We argued, and he blurted out that, you were not even my daughter. I asked if Dr Wellman was your father and he said it was somebody else who was closer than I could imagine. I'm so sorry, but he wouldn't tell me who it is.

Lia, I love you, and I hope that you will always think of me as your father, but I can't go on. When you read this, I will be dead but please don't blame yourself. Blame the people around us that have been so cruel and laughed behind our back for all of these years.

I'm so sorry my darling.

I put the letter back in the envelope.

"So is it worth a lot of money?" Asked Gilda.

"I can understand why Enrico thought so, but we are not in a position to benefit."

"Oh."

My brain was working overtime trying to piece together what the letter meant. Rico must have stolen it from Lia. Possibly the night that I picked him up on the road outside the Grange. An insurance policy does not cover suicide. If Binky had committed suicide, then nobody could have claimed anything off the insurance company, so it had to be made to look as if he had been murdered. Enrico had obviously been part of the plot to do this and must have seen a great opportunity to blackmail Alfred. But who else was in on it?

Gilda interrupted my thought pattern. "What happens when that man gets back? Do we have to give him the letter?"

"I haven't got around to thinking about that one, Gilda. You said that there were two things that Rico gave you. What's the other one?"

I heard the footsteps coming down the stairs behind the door, as I said the words. Time was running out for us, and I didn't have any plan to get us out of the mess. I watched Gilda unzip a pocket of her Parka like watching a short video play in slow motion. She pulled out a plastic bag wrapped up with scotch tape. She handed it to me, and I tore it open like a mad rabies ridden dog, with saliva dribbling down my chin, knowing that we were both probably about to be shot.

Inside the package, wrapped in a plastic bag, was a .38 pistol. Probably the one that Binky had used to commit suicide. The handle had been lovingly wrapped in a paper handkerchief, and there was tape around that too. Obviously, Cicero had wanted to preserve Binky's fingerprints. With the letter and the gun, he had Alfred and everybody involved in the scam, totally stitched up. It was either pay up or shut Rico up, and Alfred had chosen the permanent option.

I quickly took the gun out of the plastic bag and stuffed it through the belt at the back of my trousers. The door opened.

"Don't say anything, Gilda. Do you hear me?"

She nodded and shrank back in her seat.

Alfred entered the room with Sky. He had a gun in his hand.

"Awake at last, Mr Shannon. Now, I believe that you have some things that belong to me. Tell me where they are and you can be on your way."

"Do you think for a moment that I believe that? If I tell you where they are, then we are both dead."

"Really, Mr Shannon, aren't we being a bit melodramatic?"

"Why do you say that?"

"If I have the items I require, then you don't have any proof, so you can say or do what you want, and it is your word against mine. I hardly think that anybody would believe somebody with your background."

"You are a great actor, Alfred, but not too clever."

"Pray, dear boy, tell me why."

"I don't have it all worked out, but I know that your dad killed himself. I also know that there was a clause in the insurance that said it didn't pay out for suicide. I think your dad wanted to pay the lot of you back, and he almost succeeded until you had the idea to dress up as him and fake a murder. The fact that I arrived the same day it all happened could have been a tragedy, but you turned it into an advantage. By fooling me, you made the murder look even more realistic."

"I do believe that the knock on your head has done something to your brain, Mr Shannon."

"I don't think so. You see, you thought you were so clever, but you gave it all away with a misplaced sentence. I only told your dad that I was an erotic ladies underwear salesman, yet you seemed to know that when I tried to gain access to the murder scene."

"Sounds like a load of old tosh to me."

"You made the room dark and covered yourself up so I could hardly see you. You and your dad both had beards, but after we had spoken, you shaved yours off, so I didn't have a chance to recognise you."

"Look, old boy. I'm sure you believe what you say, but if you don't tell me where the letter and the gun are hidden, then I am going to start to shoot you from the bottom to the top until you do."

"Go on, darling," said Sky. "Put a bullet in his leg now, and he won't be so chirpy."

"Patience, my dear. I am going to count to five, and then I will."

I pulled the gun out and aimed it loosely in his general direction. That wiped the smile off both of their faces. Alfred recovered first, though.

"It seems Mr Shannon that we have, what they call in the old western films a Mexican..."

I shot him at the top of his thigh, and he dropped his gun and went down on the floor squealing like a pig. He should have thought himself lucky that I wasn't a very good shot as I was aiming for his balls.

Sky screamed as well, but she still tried to get to his gun before I did. I stood on her wrist and felt the satisfactory sound of it snapping under my weight.

"I think you meant to say, Mexican stand-off. Am I right, old boy?" I turned to Gilda who was staring at the scene like a rabbit caught in the headlights of a juggernaut. "It looks like they don't want to talk to me right now. Can you make yourself useful, go and find a phone and call the police."

She didn't need telling twice and practically sprinted out of the room. I sat down on the stool she had just vacated and waited.

CHAPTER TWENTY-THREE

It had been 24 hours since the arrest of Alfred and Sky Rothchester, and I was yet again pulling up to Woodley Grange for another visit. This time I was determined that it would be my last. After spending a couple of hours in the local police station giving my statement, I took Gilda back to her caravan and spent what was left of the evening back in the hotel pondering the case over a few beers and whiskies.

DCI Foxley had given me one last warning and told me to make myself scarce. I had no doubt that the plodding detective would eventually work out all the details without my help, but I had not been hired to solve a murder, and I still hadn't found out who had sent Roxy the threatening letter.

Vanessa opened the door, and when I said I wanted to see Lia, she took me to a sitting room on the second floor. She showed me in and left. Lia was sitting alone watching TV. It was one of those hysterical talk shows that seemed to fill up afternoon television schedules these days. When she saw me, she switched it off.

I called over, "Can I sit down?"

Her voice was flat and emotionless. "Hello again, Mr Shannon. Do come and join me, if you must."

I walked over and dropped into an armchair, which sent up a cloud of dust.

"Do you understand what acute suicidal depression is, Mr Shannon?"

I said I didn't.

"Neither did I until this moment. I can tell you if I had the courage of my mother, then I think this would be a good time to die."

"That's a fair point. Maybe you should consider it."

"What do you mean by that?" She met my gaze but didn't hold it for a second. "Explain yourself."

"You sent those letters to you mother. You must have hated her after reading your father's suicide note."

She dropped her head, and her shoulders sagged as if a great weight had just fallen on them. She sat there, dry-eyed and silent for what must have been a full minute. I knew this game well. The looser was the first one to speak, and there was no way it was going to be me.

"I hated them all after what they had done. Somebody had to pay, and in the end, I decided that it should be the lot."

"You gassed you grandfather."

"He was a monster, telling dad what he did. Wellman begged for mercy like a child before I shot him. I don't feel guilty. They were all scum."

"Of course they were, Lia. I don't blame you. Where were you when your dad killed himself?"

"I'm still going to call him dad, even though he wasn't. What is a dad anyway? I was in work. It had all been planned out by the time I got back. He wanted to get revenge, but they got around it, so I felt it was my duty. I know that my mum couldn't take the pressure. That was the type of person she was. Weak minded."

"Did Enrico steal the suicide note and blackmail Alfred with it?"

"Probably. I don't know."

"Do you know who your real father is?"

She shook her head and put her hands in front of her face.

I'd heard enough. I got up and made my way to the car park, feeling so glad that I was an only child.

EPILOGUE

Lia confessed the murder of her grandfather and Dr Wellman to the police later on that day. Vanessa came clean about helping Alfred, Sky, Roxy and Cicero in making Binky's death look like a suicide.

Alfred and Sky denied everything but unless they had a brilliant defence lawyer didn't stand much of a chance of getting off.

It looked as though Cicero had seen the possibility of blackmail right from the beginning. He covered the pistol with tissue paper to preserve Binky's fingerprints. He must have let himself out of the kitchen, fired the gun and then returned just in time to be sent to see what had happened. When Lia told him about the suicide note, I guess he thought that he had won first prize in the lottery. He stole the note, and the rest is history.

Alfred could have chosen to pay up but decided that getting rid of Cicero was a better option.

When I got back to Croxley, Shoddy handed me a piece of information about Sergeant Floyd, which I found extremely interesting. He had been working in Oxford at the same time that Roxy, Wellman, and Binky had been students. Was that just a coincidence? Was he Lia's real father? He was also first on the scene when the police were called the night Binky died. Who knows, maybe it was him that fired the pistol into the air. I passed on the information to Foxley to do with as he wished.

So in the end, they were all guilty and I was lucky to get out of the sleepy little village of Woodley in one piece.

I was now looking forward to dealing with some normal low-life-scum, which on balance is a lot less of a hassle than the English Aristocracy.

Roll on my next case.

The End

Thank you for reading the Penny Detective. If you enjoyed it, pass it on and tell some of your friends.

Visit my author page here: Visit Amazon's John Tallon Jones Page Click FOLLOW, and you will get up-to-date information on all future releases.

If you want to contact me with any comments, ideas or thoughts about the book, or just for a chat, look me up on:

Facebook: https://www.facebook.com/john.t.jones.52

Twitter: https://twitter.com/john151253.

Email me at john151253@gmail.com to go on my mailing list for information about new books coming out. I never divulge any information to a third party.

I always reply and am always very happy to hear from you.

Other books in the Penny Detective Series are:

1. The Penny Detective

2. The Italian Affair

Before you go, here are a couple of chapters from book 12 in the Penny Detective series; A Simple case of Murder

CHAPTER ONE

The last thing that you want when you arrive at the office on a Monday morning is somebody waiting for you by your door. He was a big man, wearing a designer electric blue double-breasted suit over a white cashmere polar neck sweater. He had pouty effeminate facial features, long blonde hair, and an ever so slight nervous tick. He wasn't the sort of client that I was used to, especially so early in the day. His suit was already giving me a headache and made me wish I had stayed in bed.

As I was unlocking the door, he stood back and looked me up and down. I could feel his light blue eyes boring into my back wondering if he had made a mistake in coming. He was acting like a first-class passenger who had drifted into economy by mistake.

I pushed the door open and said, "Good morning," without much enthusiasm.

He didn't answer but instead offered me his well-manicured hand. I expected his handshake to be feeble, but he had a grip like a pneumatic vice and the rings on all of his fingers, including his thumb, cut into me and made me wince visibly. He released my hand, put his around my shoulders, and escorted me into my office. He kicked the door closed behind us, walked over to the desk, sat down, and waited for me to do the same. I hadn't even had a chance to take off my coat, but because there was no heating, I decided to keep it on. As I sat down, he gave me another one of those searching looks, though never made direct eye contact. I hated the guy already, and he hadn't spoken a word. This was about to change, though.

"Mr Shannon?"

I was tempted to say no, just to get rid of him, but affirmed that I was with a slight nod of my head.

"Mr Shannon, I took your name out of the telephone book, I believe that you are a private detective. Is that right?"

"I am. Is there anything in particular that I can do for you, or are you just doing a job survey?" Was I being too hard on a potential client? It was hard to say, but he definitely was one of those people that gave you a natural feeling of uneasiness, and for the life of me, I didn't know why.

If the stranger was picking up any bad vibes off me, it didn't show, and my sarcasm seemed to have gone over his head, for which I was grateful.

"I have some work for you to do." He looked at my open desk diary and the two blank pages before adding. "That is if you are not too busy."

I shut the diary and waited for him to continue.

"It's probably not what someone like you would consider to be a big job, but I am willing to pay you one hundred and fifty pounds, for what will not be more than a day's work."

"Add expenses on top of that, and you have got yourself a deal."

"Expenses?"

"Yeah, like travel, food, and extras."

"Extras?"

I passed him my terms and conditions. "Extras are marked down under miscellaneous.

He studied the paper for the briefest of moments and passed it back to me with a wry smirk. "That seems to be in order, Mr Shannon. So it's one hundred and fifty pounds plus extras." He looked at me full in the face for the first time. Up close I could see that there were dark lines under his eyes and that his skin, which had looked faultless, had several spots and pockmarks. He had tried to cover them up with blusher, which said a lot about what sort of a man he was. Certainly, a vain one by the immaculate way he was dressed, and certainly a rich one too if he was prepared to pay me that much for a day's work. I was intrigued, and as always, desperate for cash, so for me it was a win, win, which made a change. I was mentally tapping my fingers while I waited for the catch. In my life, there always was one.

"So can you give me a few details?"

"Yes I can, Mr Shannon. My name is Kristian Bruce, but you can call me Kris. Everybody else does.

"Do you live in Croxley, Mr Bruc?"

"For the purpose of the job I want you to do, it isn't any concern of yours where I live. The way I thought it worked with you type of people was you get told what to do and just do it."

I reached for a pen and made a show out of writing on my notepad, his name, and underneath; 'no address given.' I underlined the second fact twice.

"Shall I be blunt?"

"Yeah, why don't you?"

"I'm finding your tone since I arrived to be more than a little aggressive. Do you want this job or are you insisting on talking yourself out of it? Is my money not good enough for you?"

"To be fair, Kris, I haven't seen any money yet, so I can't comment."

He took the hint, produced a red leather wallet, counted out one hundred pounds in tens, and handed them to me. "There you go. Does that buy me a bit of respect as well as your time?"

"A retainer does go a long way to establish a certain bond between master and servant, Kris. Will you be needing a receipt?"

He shook his head and went back to looking everywhere except me. I suspected from experience that this was because he was either about to tell me a pack of lies, or lay a job on me that was highly dangerous and worth more than he was paying.

I gave him a verbal nudge. "I'll do most things, Kris, as long as they are not illegal. Does that make sense?"

"What do you take me for? I'm certainly not suggesting you do something that is not completely above board."

"OK, Kris, just tell me in your own time what it is that you want me to do."

He reached into his suit brought out a cigarette and inserted it into his mouth. Thankfully he didn't light it but placed an expensive looking Zippo in front of him in anticipation. Was it to be a lie, illegal, or very dangerous? That was the burning question, and the suspense was murdering me.

Finally, he was ready, and he focused on the ceiling above my head. "I want you to find someone for me. A man who used to be my employee. My chauffeur, actually. He went out shopping a couple of weeks ago, and didn't come back."

"So what's the problem? Why don't you just get a new one? There are plenty of people out there looking for work with clean driving licenses."

"That may well be the case, Mr Shannon, but when he left he took my BMW Series 5 with him, and I'd rather like it back."

"Are you insured?"

"It's a bit more complicated than that."

"It sounds like you should go and talk to the police. He could be anywhere by now."

"I don't think so. Like I said, it's a bit more complicated than just a straight theft of a motor car. The truth is, Mr Shannon, I had a very genuine affection for Winston. I get rather attached to the people that work for me, and now I feel a bit guilty."

"Go on."

"Winston was my chauffeur for about eighteen months. I knew that he had a gambling habit and I gave him money occasionally to pay off his debts. I think those debts got a bit too big for him in the end, and he was forced to disappear."

Pack of lies it was then! I'd imagine a snake had more compassion than this guy, but I needed the money, and that was staying put in my pocket.

He locked eye contact and put on his most compassionate face. I could almost hear schmaltzy violins in the background.

"If Winston has left Merseyside, Kris, it could take considerably longer than a day to find him."

"Winston has left Merseyside for sure, but I know where he is."

"So if you know where he is, then why not go and talk to him yourself?"

"That's exactly what I intend to do, right after you fulfill your side of the job."

"And what is my side of the job?"

"I think that Winston is in trouble, Mr Shannon. I think he has got in with the wrong crowd, but until I know who they are, I can't help him. I simply want you to follow him for a day, find out where he is living, and make a note of the people he sees."

"Isn't that a bit of an elaborate way to go about recovering your car?"

"That is none of your business, but I will say, that I do have a certain number of connections in the right places that could help Winston, but I know he would never allow it. That's why I need you to be as discreet as possible. You can be discreet, Mr Shannon?"

"Oh I can be discreet alright, but I need to know where to find him first. Are you going to tell me, or do I have to guess?"

"He's in Salford, which is near Manchester. Do you know it?"

"I know of it, but I can't say that I've ever had the pleasure of visiting the area. How are you so sure that he's there?"

"I know this because a friend of mine saw my car on two occasions parked outside a cafe and phoned me. He was a bit shocked knowing my views on style when it comes to eating out. I got him to talk to a waiter, and it seems that Winston has been a regular over the last few weeks. I guess I should have known that he would return to his roots. He is a Salford lad, so I suppose he feels safe there. It's a greasy spoon cafe called The Pancake Kitchen." He handed me a piece of paper with the address written on it.

"Have you got a picture?"

"I haven't, but he shouldn't be too hard to identify. He is Jamaican, about the same height as you with long hair done the way that they all do it out there. I can't remember what they call it."

"Dreadlocks."

"Yes, that's the word. He has got those dreadlock things down his back. He was a bodyguard as well as a chauffeur. Just looking at him would scare people away."

"So he's a big man with Bob Marley type hair. Is that correct."

"I suppose so. Who is Bob Marley?"

"He was a Jamaican singer."

"I'm afraid, Mr Shannon that my musical tastes stop at Frank Sinatra. Was this Bob Marley anything like him?"

"Yeah sort of, but anyway I've got a picture in my mind's eye of what I'm looking out for. What is the registration of the BMW?

He wasn't expecting that but recovered. "Yes, it's KB 1."

"Personalized?"

"Is there any other sort of number plate?"

"Does Winston have a second name?"

"Yes, it's Winston Moon."

I wrote the name down as he was getting up out of his chair. "So do you understand what you have to do, Mr Shannon?"

"Clear as day, Kris. I go to Salford and sniff around the cafe he was last seen in. If I get lucky, I follow him; find out where he lives, and who he talks to. I make sure I don't get seen, then report back to you. Shall I come to your house?"

"There is my home telephone number underneath the address of the cafe. Give me a call when you have any information."

With that, he walked out of the door without as much as a goodbye and good luck. You get a feel for clients over the years. The feeling I had about Kris Bruce was that he was a bullshitter that had just told me a pack of lies. Whatever his motive was for contacting his ex-chauffeur, my gut feeling told me that it wasn't out of a heartfelt kindness. Did I care one way or the other? On the surface, it looked easy money, but in this job, you could never be certain.

I got up and walked over to the window. On the High Street below, Kris had just emerged. I watched as he strode purposely through the early morning shoppers. He didn't fit into this sleazy part of town, and his suit pulled in a few knowing glances and sly smirks.

I waited till he was just an electric blur on the horizon, got my hat and coat, and made my way to the pub before the money burnt a hole through my pocket.

CHAPTER TWO

The journey from Croxley to Salford would have taken a normal car under an hour, but my vehicle didn't fit into that category. I suppose that the Riley Elf was considered to be an OK ride when it first came off the production line in the late 1960s. Almost twenty years later, my particular Elf is still technically roadworthy, but the engine complains bitterly about going any distance greater than a couple of miles.

I was on the M62, desperately looking for a turn off for the M 602. From behind the oil tanker, I was following, the visibility was worrying and the rolling early morning fog wasn't helping. The truth is that after Kris had left me, I had headed to the pub and stayed there all day with my best friend and business partner Shoddy. We continued in party mode back at his flat like a couple of teenagers, and I had woken up with a banging hangover a couple of hours later.

On either side of the motorway, I was on; there was very little in the way of picturesque bliss. Just endless fields full of sheep or rapeseed, and the occasional industrial eyesore that blotted the landscape and belched out strange coloured orange or grey smoke.

There were no hills here or pleasant valleys covered with lush orchards. The road to Salford was devoid of beauty, and the clean air had been sucked up and replaced with a dangerous chemical cocktail that filled your lungs and made you wish that you were somewhere else. This road was about as bad as driving in the North of England gets, and I had chosen the scenic route on my partner's advice. It beggared belief what the un-scenic route looked like.

The Elf stumbled onto the 602 and spewed itself out onto the A5063, which was the main drag into Salford itself. I was passing decrepit looking two up two down townhouses now, sitting next door to huge faceless warehouses that looked like abandoned aircraft hangers. No happy smiling stream of workers graced these doors anymore. Any chance of work in this suburb had disappeared a long time ago. Jobs had left the piss poor streets of Salford and the vacuum produced had brought in all of the scum of the universe.

I pulled into a Shell Garage and asked directions for Fitzwarren Street, and the Pancake Kitchen. There was no love lost between the people of Salford and Liverpool, and when the young scally behind the counter heard my accent, he just shrugged and started talking to somebody else. I didn't push it because if I had, he would have probably been able to rustle up a few mates from the car repair centre next door, to give me a good kicking. It was that type of vibe all around me. I decided to keep my mouth shut and not eyeball anybody under the age of 75. The whole issue was bound up with soccer and the rivalry between the fans, and who could blame them. There was nothing else to occupy what was left of their minds in this shit hole.

I eventually found a quiet looking window cleaner that was willing to speak to me, and he pointed me in the right direction. The further you got into the centre of town, the more you realised you were glad to live in another neighbourhood. There was no rich, poor divide here, just poor, and it showed on the faces of the people shuffling themselves about on the sidewalks. They were window-shopping where most of the windows were either boarded up or reinforced with wire mesh. The irony of it all was lost on them but not on smart-arsed me, though I wasn't laughing that much. I noticed that the majority of retailers that were open sold alcohol. Even this early in the day, youths hung around on street corners dealing in everything from crack cocaine to car radios. The police just let them get on with it, and rightly so. It was the same where I lived in Croxley. We were all fast becoming a working class tribe, without the work or the class, and the dope and drink were revolving doors that always brought us back to the same place in the cold light of morning.

There was a slight drizzle of rain that wasn't heavy enough for an umbrella but got you sufficiently wet to be uncomfortable. Fitzwarren Street was drab, depressing, and scant of people. The traffic wasn't exactly bumper-to-bumper either. I eased my way into a space behind a very old Ford something-or-other, and a clapped out Renault 5 and got out.

A policeman appeared from nowhere, like a rabbit out of a hat and looked strangely out of place. I was tempted to ask him where the cafe was, but fell into step a little way behind and did some window-shopping of my own. The Pancake House was next to a second-hand bargain store and looked a lot less impressive than it sounded. It had a wooden front that had been painted badly, and the wire mesh on the window was a substitute rather than a protection, as the glass must have been kicked in a long time ago. It was probably a very draughty place to eat breakfast, but on closer inspection, I noticed that there was a see-through polythene sheet pulled and nailed taught over the gap to keep the wind and rain out. Surprisingly, inside was crowded, so I assumed it was either cheap, or the food was good.

It was like stepping back into a post-war Russian soup kitchen. A blackboard was propped up at the side of the door offering all day breakfast and real coffee, plus lunch specials for under a pound. I dreaded to think what meat they were using. I walked into a pub that was directly opposite, ordered a beer, and settled down by the window to watch. There was no sign of the BMW, but I now understood why any friend of Kris would have spotted it when it was parked outside because it would have stood out like a nun in a brothel. I looked at my watch. It was coming up to one o'clock. Lunchtime! I wondered if today was going to be lucky. At two o'clock I was still wondering, and at half past two I was ready to go home, and feeling more than a bit drunk.

I had sat by the window and watched a mostly downtrodden clientele come and go through the steamed-up glass door of the Pancake House. The flashiest car I had seen so far was a clapped out Escort. I drained my beer and got up, with a rough idea to tour the area looking for anybody that had dreadlocks.

As I hit the street, a huge gorilla of a man with dreadlocks walked past me and headed for the cafe. I'm six feet four, and my size often turns heads when I walk into a bar or a public area. This guy was not only my size with the right shade of skin colour but also had the hairstyle I was looking for. He was wearing a multi-coloured shell suit jacket, jogging pants, and trainers. He disappeared into the cafe, and I went back into the pub to wait for him to come out.

He couldn't have had much of an appetite because he reappeared after about ten minutes and headed off the way he had come when he arrived. I exited the pub and was halfway down the street when he got to the corner. He turned right, and I caught up and settled down a little way behind, but almost having to jog to keep up.

There was an aggressive aura about Winston, and Kris wasn't lying about him looking scary. There was no sign of a BMW, which was fortunate because if he had got into one, I was so far from my car that I would have lost him.

We walked the poverty-stricken backstreets of Salford for about twenty minutes and eventually came to a canal that blocked the way. Winston again turned right and then a quick left into a road signposted Beasley Street. The road was cobbled and full of young kids who were mostly kicking balls around in the mud and grime. The houses here left a lot to be desired and could have been empty for all the signs of life. Some of the windows had been broken and patched up with gaffer tape and cardboard, and most of the doors had the scars of degradation and violent behaviour. One or two houses didn't have any doors at all and had been boarded up and left to fester and die. Winston ignored the squalor he was passing through as if he had seen it all before. At the end of Beasley Street, we came to a road that was normal and with houses that could have passed the definition of what homes should look like. These small pearls had well-kept gardens and proper windows and doors. It was into one of these gardens he turned. He walked up the path, past a decrepit metallic blue Mini. I tried to make myself look invisible and kept well back. I needn't have bothered because Winston wasn't taking any notice of anything. I began to wonder if he was stoned. I made a note of the house number.

The door opened before he had chance to knock. At the distance, I was standing I could just about make out a man silhouetted in the doorframe. He looked old enough to be his dad, but as Winston entered, the man squeezed his bottom and stuck a huge pink tongue in his ear which didn't look that parental even to someone as naive as me. If Winston was shocked, he didn't show it. The door slammed shut as if they were in a hurry, and I looked around the street to see if there was a good place to watch the house without being seen.

Made in the USA
Middletown, DE
12 July 2021

44026577R00139